CW01401838

Carnal
Persuasion

Severed MC Book Four

by

K.T. Fisher

and

Ava Manello

*Nikki
Hope you
enjoy the Nic
Severed Gang
Saga*

K.T. Fisher

Ava Manello x

Lisa Marie ♡

(handwritten signatures)

Copyright

K.T. Fisher and Ava Manello
Carnal Persuasion

© 2014, K.T. Fisher and Ava Manello

KBK Publishing

ISBN-13: 978-1503304956

ISBN-10: 1503304957

Cover Model: Asher Collins

Cover Photographer: RIHUPHOTO

Cover Designer: Margreet Asselbergs

CARNAL PERSUASION (SEVERED MC #4)

DEDICATION

When we sat down to decide who we should dedicate this book to, we actually said the same thing at the same time.

So this book is dedicated to our readers, who have followed us faithfully from that first chapter in Severed Angel and survived right through to the torture that we put them through in Severed Justice.

Thank you for your support, for loving our characters as much as we do and for your kind and thoughtful messages as you're reading or finished reading a book. Even if some of them do include a fair few cuss words.

We hope that you enjoy this next installment in the Severed MC series.

K.T and Ava

Prologue

Cowboy

It's dark when I let myself into Emma's apartment. Even if everything has gone to plan, I know it will be tomorrow before she gets back.

I shouldn't have let her embark on this crazy scheme of hers on her own. But, she was so determined; nothing and no one could sway her from her path.

I sink into her sofa, guilt eating away at me.

I'm carrying a shit load of guilt around with me these days. Guilt that I've let Emma go in search of a madman, guilt that I didn't rush into that cabin in time, guilt that I sat there in the shop whilst Danni died just feet away, guilt for not getting to

Cassie quickly enough and even more guilt that in my stupid ignorance I hadn't realized she was still alive when I got there.

There's so much guilt it feels like a fucking cancer, destroying me from the inside out.

I sit there in the darkness, alone. I feel so fucking alone all the time now, even when I'm in a crowd of people. Emma's spent the last three months focused on revenge. It's the only thing that's kept her going. It was the reason she needed to get out of bed in the morning. I don't have a focus and I sure as shit don't have a reason for getting out of bed anymore.

This is a dangerous time of night. The time between midnight and dawn. It's the time where I let the dark thoughts take over. Would anyone miss me if I were gone? I really don't think they would. I think they'd be better off if I wasn't here. I'm just a dead weight now.

I've lost weight. My jeans and shirt hang from my hollow frame. I have no interest in eating. I've been keeping my own company most of the time. Not that anyone's really noticed; they're all so busy living their own lives, as they should.

The last three months, hell, the last six months, have been the scariest that most of us have lived through. We've been hunted, betrayed and picked off, one by one. I'm such a selfish prick I didn't notice when my best friend was falling apart and turning into a rat. How could I not see the hell that he was going through? Perhaps though, he just learned to hide it well. A skill I've come to master myself of late.

I try to think of anyone who'd be better off with me in their life and I'm sad to say that I can't. Sure, a few people would shed tears if I wasn't around anymore, but they'd soon pick up and move on with their lives. Angel has Eve and Elizabeth. Prez has Teresa and they're expecting a baby. Emma's going to move on with her own life once tonight's over. Come tomorrow, she won't need me anymore.

I understand now what I have to do. It's like a fog has lifted, revealing the clear path lying ahead of me.

I turn the polished metal in my hands. Such a small thing, yet it can destroy so many lives. Tonight though I'm going to use it to make other people's lives better. That's got to be a good thing. Right?

I place the barrel of the gun in my mouth, closing my lips around it. Am I supposed to say a prayer now? Make a peace with my God?

The problem is I no longer have faith. How can you watch so many people you love die and still have faith in a religion?

It's selfish of me to do this here. It's not fair on Emma. She's tough though. She'll handle it. She'll get over it.

Spinning the barrel, I leave the decision to fate. Bracing myself, I pull the trigger. The click of the gun masking the soft click of the door opening.

Russian fucking roulette. The pull of the trigger is the only noise the gun makes. Fate has decided. She's not done with me yet.

Chapter One

Lucy

I'm standing in the doorway, numbed by the sight in front of me. For a moment I can't bring myself to move, then the reality of the situation hits me and I run screaming into the room.

"No!" I scream as I run at Cowboy. It's probably not the wisest thing to do when he's holding a gun in his mouth, but I'm too shocked to be capable of rational thought right now.

It's obviously enough to startle him, as he lowers his hand and looks at me. Shock is written across his features. This isn't the Cowboy I know. He's become a shadow of himself the past few months, from what Emma has told me, even back when I first met him, he was a different man from who he used to be.

I know from the things I've heard that he's had a really bad time of it, the whole of Severed has. When I look into his deep brown eyes there's no life reflecting back at me. It's like looking into deep pools of darkness. No emotion at all.

There's the subtlest movement in his shoulders, then he breaks down, crying. Fuck. What am I supposed to do? I can barely handle it when Emma cries. I'm not someone who's comfortable with emotions. I've no idea how to comfort a man.

I move to sit beside him on the sofa, carefully removing the gun from his hand, moving it out of his reach. I hate the feel of the gun, it's cold, hard metal. I hate what it represents even more though.

I sit there uncomfortably, reaching for his hand. His hands are large and strong. They're what this man is all about. His tattoos reach all the way down his arms, covering the back of his hands with their intricate designs. Unconsciously I trace my finger across the back of one. It's enough for him to notice that I'm here. In a move that's too quick for me to realize, he's lifted me from the seat and drawn me onto his lap. My head fits just under his neck and he cradles me to his body, his head on mine and his hand stroking my hair. He continues to sob, but his chest is heaving less now and it's becoming quieter.

"Why?" I whisper to him. "Why would you do this to us, to Emma, to your friends?"

His deep voice is slow to reply and slightly broken when he does. "Because you'd all be better off without me." He's so serious when he says it that my heart breaks a little.

I get that I didn't meet him at his best, but for the several months that I've known him, he's been like a big, cuddly bear. He's always watched out for Emma and I, been there whenever we needed anything, I can't imagine him not being part of our lives anymore.

He's big and strong and, if I'm honest, bloody good looking as well. He's got short dark hair, stubble that's grown out into a short beard and the darkest eyes I've ever seen. And when he smiles. God that smile could melt a snowman's heart.

I try and remember when I last saw him smile. I realize that I can't. When was the last time the light shone in his eyes?

"No we wouldn't." I look up at him as I speak. "We'd all be lost without you." I tell him.

He looks at me, disbelief written across his face. "You stupid, stupid man." I continue. "You really don't get it do you?" He watches me carefully as I talk.

"You have so many friends and we wouldn't be the same if we lost you. You're important to us. You hold us together. We won't let you go."

"I'm sorry." He whispers back. I'm not sure if I've convinced him how much he means to us all, but he holds me a little tighter. We sit there like that, silently, until the sun rises.

Chapter Two

Cowboy

I can't believe what I tried to do last night. I know I was in a bad place, but not that I'd sunk that low.

Would I have tried again if Lucy hadn't walked in on me? I'm not sure. What I do know is that she got to me last night and that I won't be trying it again.

At some point Lucy fell asleep in my arms; holding her felt so right that I didn't want to wake her. It was good to hold someone close. I've never had that special person in my life. I'm a biker, all I know are the other guy's old ladies or a bunch of club whores.

I'm too broken to be loved, or to love someone back, although I want to. One day I'd like to have what Angel, Prez and Ink have. I'm just not sure I'm capable of it. A woman deserves the best, a guy who'll wine her and dine her, who'll romance the shit out of her. I don't think I could be that man.

The sun rising through the window wakes Lucy. She stretches her back like a cat, smiling cautiously at me when she notices I'm still holding her close. I don't want to let her go.

"Morning, Cowboy." Her voice is gentle and warm.

"Morning sweetheart." Her face lights up in a smile.

"Now there's the Cowboy we all know and love."

"Look, Lucy. About last night..." She cuts me off before I can finish.

"We're not going to talk about it." She declares, her words firm and strong. "We're going to forget it happened.' She smirks at me before continuing. "Apart from the cuddling me all night, I want to remember that." She blushes as she finishes.

"Deal." I offer.

"You want coffee?" She's already moved from my lap and heading to the kitchen area.

"Please. Black, no sugar."

While Lucy busies herself in the kitchen I see an envelope on the coffee table with my name on it. Curious, I pick it up and open it.

Cowboy,

By the time you read this, I'll have served my Justice. I can't thank you enough for being there for me the last three months, it's been hell, but you made it a little easier.

I know you don't agree with what I've done. Will it help set the ghosts to rest, or make me feel better? I don't know. I can only hope so.

Now, I need to go away. I need to be selfish, to do this for me. I can't stay in Severed. There are too many memories, too many ghosts. I need to go and start afresh, build a new life for my baby.

I'll be in touch when I'm settled, let you know where I am. Give me time, please don't look for me.

I need one more favor from you. I need you to watch over Lucy. I know she'll worry about me, but I know with you keeping an eye on her she'll be fine.

Tell her I'm sorry. I couldn't face any more goodbyes right now.

Emma

xxx

I lean back against the sofa. "Shit." I thought I'd said that in my head, but from the way Lucy just looked up, she heard me.

"What's wrong?" She looks nervous again. I hold up the piece of paper in my hand.

"It's a letter from Emma. She's not coming back." Lucy's face falls. Shit. Perhaps a little more tact would have been appropriate.

"What do you mean? She wouldn't leave us, not when she's expecting the baby and everything. She needs us." I'm not sure if Lucy is trying to convince herself or me here.

"Here, read it for yourself." I hand the note over and watch as Lucy's face falls. I'm not convinced Emma has done the best thing here, but part of me understands why. It's hard being left behind, when every time you turn a corner or open a door, you're reminded of the people that aren't there anymore.

I look around the room and in the light of day see what I missed last night. Emma's gone. The little knick-knacks and girly shit are missing. The apartment looks bare and empty without them.

Lucy falls into the space beside me on the sofa, her hand over her mouth as she continues to read her best friends farewell. Once again I find myself pulling Lucy into my arms. This time she's the one crying. Shit. I even feel guilty for this. It's my fault that Emma's gone. I should have taken better care of her, I should have stopped her going ahead with her stupid plan.

Lucy looks at me and it's as though she can read my mind. "Don't you dare feel responsible for this. She's a grown woman. She's left both of us. I'm just as much to blame as you are." She sobs again.

"It's okay Lucy, sweetheart. I'm here for you." I offer as I hold her close.

She doesn't realize it, but I'm going to honor Emma's request. I'm going to keep my eye on Lucy for her. I'm not about to lose anyone else that I care about.

As I stand there holding Lucy close, my resolve returns. I'm done with feeling sorry for myself. This shit stops now.

Chapter Three

Lucy

I didn't sleep well last night. I guess it was shock at finding Cowboy like that, my best friend leaving and the stress over losing my job. I didn't tell Cowboy about that, if he found out how I lost it I know he'd go mental and try and fix it for me. I reckon he's got enough stress of his own anyway, without adding my problems to the mix.

Tossing and turning all night meant I had plenty of time to think about my future. I'm not going to get a reference from my old boss, that's for sure, so that really limits the options I have open to me. The only idea I've come up with is to go check out the help wanted sign at the bar where Danni used to work at. I feel slightly uncomfortable with the idea; I'd hate anyone to think I was stepping in her shoes. No one ever could, everyone round here loved that girl, but I really don't have any other choice right now.

A hot and steamy shower calms me slightly. I dress in my denim skirt and white vest top, scooping my hair into a loose bun on top of my head because today is supposed to be a scorcher. Sipping on my shoes, I take one last look in the mirror to see if I look the part before leaving the house. It's certainly not what I'd wear for an office job, but it should pass for a barmaid.

I stand outside the bar still wondering if this is the right thing to do. Since I really need a new job, it's a no brainer. I take a deep breath and go to open the door, but slam into the wood instead. I frown at the locked door, pressing my ear against it. I can hear men's voices inside and lots of banging. What the hell is happening in there?

I bang on the door so they can hear me over the noise inside. Why would the bar be shut at this time of the day? It's only then I notice the other sign – 'closed for refurbishment'.

The door opens suddenly, snapping me from my thoughts and I find myself staring into the bright blue eyes of a sexy stranger. This guy is gorgeous; I almost bite down on my lip thanks to the naughty thoughts running through my mind. He's dressed in just jeans and work boots, his hot sweaty chest at eye level with me. *Holy shit.*

"Can I help you?" He asks sounding a little bored, as he looks me up and down.

"Erm," I stutter. I really need to collect my thoughts. "Hi, I'm here for the job?"

"Oh." He looks me over again, as though I'm some investment he's about to take a chance on. I must pass his invisible test because he nods his head and finally smiles at me. Damn that's one sexy smile. "Have you done any bar work before?"

"A little." I lie. "More waitressing though." Not totally true, but I have helped out at my parents from time to time when they hosted a party.

The stranger smiles. I have the sneaky suspicion he knows that I'm not being completely honest. He takes a step back, inviting me in with his outstretched hand. "I'm Declan, the new owner of this place."

"Hi Declan, I'm Lucy. I didn't know the bar was up for sale."

"An old friend owned it and made me an offer I couldn't refuse. I needed a career change." I take in his solid body and prominent abs, wondering what he used to do. My brain is obviously not in sync with my mouth as I've blurted the question out loud without meaning to.

"I came here to start a new future, not discuss my past." He states, his tone closed off and denying me the opportunity to ask further questions.

"A new future sounds pretty good to me right now as well." I say instead.

CARNAL PERSUASION (SEVERED MC #4)

A loud bang quite close to us makes me jump. Declan laughs. "Sorry, I'm having the place refurbished. You want to walk with me while I check on stuff, that way I can show you around whilst giving you a quick interview." He has a mesmerizing voice.

"Sure." I agree as I look around the bar area. Everything looks much more modern, even though it's not finished yet I can tell I'm going to love it.

Declan starts to show me around as he asks his questions, which don't really amount to much. He asks about my previous work experience. I haven't had a lot of jobs, so it doesn't take long to come round to my last position as a receptionist.

"Why did you leave?" He asks me as he shows me the new staff room.

"I didn't exactly leave." He turns and gives me a questioning look. "I was fired."

Declan looks shocked for about a second, then smirks down at me. "How could someone fire a little thing like you?"

"Little?" I bite back. I'm five foot seven, hardly little, but I guess next to this guy who towers over me I would appear small.

"Don't take offense Lucy, I just meant that you don't seem like the type of girl to cause trouble."

"I'm not." Declan continues to look at me, it's a valid question so I answer it honestly. "I slapped my boss because he was a little too friendly."

Declan's face instantly darkens. "By friendly do you mean inappropriate behavior?"

I nod. "Yeah, he was always like that. I'd learned to deal with it, until he cornered me in his office." I feel dirty just thinking about it.

"Men like him piss me off." He growls. Seeing my worried face he quickly reassures me. "You don't need to worry about anything like that with me Lucy. I treat all my employees with the respect they deserve."

"It's fine." I smile up at him. Declan returns to showing me around the newly decorated bar.

I'm really impressed with what I've seen and can't wait to see the finished result. It doesn't look anything like the old bar. No doubt will bring in a new crowd. I'm pleased when Declan tells me that he's also fitting a shiny new dance floor. The girls will freak out, we loved hanging out here before, but now that it's spanking new and modern I know they'll love it as much as I do. I'm not quite so sure how the bikers will like it though. This was kind of their regular hang out away from the clubhouse.

After checking out the new kitchen and bathrooms, we're back in the main bar area when Declan turns to look at me. "I think it's safe to say you have the job, Lucy."

"Really?" I beam.

"Yeah." He laughs. "You're the only girl to come forward. You can only have so many men working here ya know. We could do with some pretty faces around here." He gives me a wink that makes me blush.

Hearing that I'm the first woman to apply is a surprise to me, but I'm also grateful, as it means I got the job.

"Thank you so much." I smile.

"For the job or saying that you have a pretty face?"

"The job." I blush again. Damn, is he going to affect me like this while we're working? He's such a charmer, good looking with it as well.

"No problem. We're scheduled to open next Friday, but I d like you to start on Wednesday to help set everything up and meet the others."

"That's fine by me."

He grins and places his hand on my shoulder, guiding me to the door. "Great, I'll see you 11:00am Wednesday morning, Lucy."

Declan flashes me one last panty-dropping smile before closing the door, leaving me feeling slightly light headed. I can't wait to tell the girls all about my new boss.

Chapter Four

Eve

I look at Gabe in disbelief. I can't believe he's just suggested that.

"You're going to teach me to ride your bike?" I repeat.

"Hell no woman, I love my bike!" He exclaims with a loud laugh. "I'm going to teach you to ride A bike." He stresses the word A.

"Oh". I'm not sure I want to learn how to ride a bike. Don't get me wrong, I love riding on the back of Gabe's bike, holding him close and feeling his lean body, but I'm not convinced giving me a bike of my own is such a great idea. I can't even handle a bicycle confidently.

"The thing is Gabe, I'm much happier on four wheels."

He doesn't say anything, but the sorrowful look on his face convinces me that I at least need to give this a go, even if the thought of it scares the shit out of me. It's not fair to him if I don't at least try. Hell, his whole life revolves around bikes and Severed MC.

I let out a heavy sigh. "Okay, fine." Gabe instantly smiles and I realize that he's tricked me; he knows I can't resist those damn puppy dog eyes of his.

We're in the yard at the clubhouse, in front of the bike shed. I'm not convinced this is the best place for me to learn; there are too many bikers here who would be only too happy to take the piss out of me if I made a mistake. Correct that, *when* I make a mistake, because it's inevitable isn't it? At least the yard is empty this early in the morning so there's no one to witness my embarrassment when it all goes wrong.

Gabe leads a bike out towards me. In my ignorance I can't tell you what it is, it's black and chromed and looks a lot smaller than the bikes the guys ride. I'm quite pleased to see that it has a few bumps and scrapes on it already. At least I don't have to worry about damaging the thing.

He starts to talk me through the various parts of the bike. I can feel my eyes glaze over. I have no idea what he's talking about, but decide to keep quiet. When he gets to the handlebars he confuses me even more by telling me that what I mistook for a brake is actually the clutch. I had enough trouble finding the biting point on the clutch in my bloody car, without them locating it on a bike where it looks like it should be a brake. I can tell this is not going to go well for me.

"So if that's not the brake, where is the brake?" I ask. Gabe gives me the look that tells me he's already said this once and I wasn't listening. Oops, maybe I should be paying more attention.

"The brake is under your right foot." He looks down at the boots on my feet and grimaces. "Baby. We need to get you some riding boots," he states.

"What's wrong with my boots?" I sulk. I love these boots. They're my biker chick boots, all leather, buckles and straps, then I realize, all heels too. They're won't be very practical when it comes to braking; the heel is a stiletto and will get in the way. Now I really don't want to learn to ride if it means wearing boots with chunky flat heels.

Gabe tells me that the next thing I need to learn is how to get the bike off its kickstand. He does it with such ease I'm shocked by how difficult it is when I attempt it. The bike weighs a ton. There's no way my small frame is going to be able to shift this hulk of metal. Gabe repeats the maneuver again.

"Try and rock the bike forward as you do it." He suggests. I try again. I fail again. I haven't even made it onto the bike yet.

"Your heart's not in this." Gabe mutters and I detect a slight tone of frustration. What can I say? He's right.

I sidle up to him. "I guess I'm just not in the mood for it this morning." I whisper seductively in his ear. That gets his attention.

"What are you in the mood for then?" He smirks.

"You." I bite down on my lip. "Let's go to your room and you can give me a lesson in riding you." Because he still has hold of the bike by its handlebars I reach down and grab his crotch, then turn and run for the clubhouse. I can hear him growling behind me.

"Woman, you'll be the death of me." He laughs as he follows me inside.

Chapter five

Cowboy

I'm sitting in Ink's tattoo shop, debating whether I should get another tattoo and trying to piss him off as much as I can when my phone rings. It's Angel

"What's up VP?" I answer. Ink moves closer to listen in on the conversation, nosey fucker.

"Cowboy? Where are you at?" Angel asks.

"Ink's shop, why?"

"You know where Prez is at?"

"My guess is with his old lady." I offer. I haven't seen him since yesterday.

I hear Angel grunt on the other end of the phone. "I'm on my way to you, is Ink there? We need to talk.'

I hang up the phone and turn to face Ink. "He's on his way."

As it's late afternoon the shop is empty when Angel pulls up in front, along with Kid and Ice.

When he strolls inside, he doesn't look happy at all. "You tried to get a hold of Prez?" He asks us. I shake my head.

"No answer " I reply with a smirk. We *all* know that if Prez doesn't answer his phone that he's probably having quality time with Teresa. Unless you want your head bitten off, you don't interrupt them.

"What's up, VP?" Ink asks.

"That damn woman of mine has tired me out too much to deal with this shit today." He groans.

Kid laughs behind him. "Eve's been learning how to ride a bike."

We all laugh as Angel rolls his eyes. "Yeah well, that bike wasn't the only thing she was riding this morning." He smirks back at us.

Ice shakes his head in disgust. "Yeah, I heard."

Poor fucker, he has the room next door to Angel's at the clubhouse and would have heard the whole thing. I look at my VP and have the feeling his old lady isn't the reason he's looking stressed.

"What's bothering you, Angel?" I ask him.

Angel runs his hands through his blonde hair in clear frustration. "I wanted to let Prez know first, but seeing as I can't get hold of him, I'll bring you in." He lets out a long sigh before continuing. "I got a phone call earlier from the manager of the strip club on the edge of town. He seems to think that we've been supplying his dancers with drugs. One of them died from an overdose last night."

"Fuck!" Ice shouts.

"He's not the only one." Angel adds.

"What the fuck?" I ask.

Angel nods. "Yeah, shortly after that call I received another that was pretty similar. I told them both we don't do drugs and we'll look into it. I thought we'd made it clear to everyone in Severed, there's no drugs allowed here."

"You don't think this could be Carnal do you, VP?" Ice asks.

Angel quickly shakes his head. "Can't be, we're pretty good with them right now. Even when we weren't they never did drugs in our backyard."

It's true, as fucked up as things were with Carnal when Satan was around, they made sure not to bring their shit here. They handled most of their business well away from Severed and still do.

"So this means it's someone new behind the drugs." I point out.

"Shit!" Ink curses. "Just as we think shit is settling down, we find ourselves right back in the thick of it."

Angel nods. He's starting to put his leather gloves back on when Kids phone starts to ring. Being as we're all nosy fuckers we listen in.

"Yo?" He answers, frowning almost right away. Whatever's being said on the other end can't be good.

"I'm with Angel now, I'll tell him."

He hangs up his phone and scrubs the back of his neck. "That was weird."

"What?" Angel asks him, looking tense.

"That was Dragon." Kid replies. "Him and Cherry went to the bar in town, the one where Danni used to work and he said it was all locked up. There's a sign on the door asking for new staff, saying it's closed for refurbishment before opening under new management."

"What the fuck?" I ask.

This can't be good, not to mention it's too much of a coincidence. We suddenly have drugs being dealt in our town; right at the same time the bar gets taken over by someone new.

Angel puts his sunglasses back on, then looks around us all. "Let's go tell Prez boys. This shit is getting deep." Pointing to Kid he tells him to get Dragon and Cherry back to the clubhouse before turning to me and Ink. "You guys need to lock up and get back, we need to call Church on this one."

Life just got weird again. I hope it's not as bad as I fear. I'm not sure I can handle any more fucked up shit after the last few months.

Chapter six

Lucy

I'm in the clubhouse yard with Eve and Elizabeth when we hear the rumble of bikes. Elizabeth starts jumping up and down singing *Daddy* as they ride in.

As we watch them, Eve turns to look at me and I know what she's thinking. I haven't known these people for more than a few months, but it's long enough to know how things go around here. Something's wrong.

Usually when the guys get off their bikes, they're all smiles and swagger. Today they turn away from their bikes with faces like thunder. Angel stops next to Elizabeth, kisses her on the head, greets me with a quick hello, then kisses Eve and lets her know he's got to go inside and deal with some club business. She nods her head in agreement.

When I spot Cowboy, I give him a questioning look, but he shakes his head and walks right by me. That tells me that this is something really important; Cowboy doesn't usually brush me off like that. I'm disappointed; I'd come to see him to tell him about my new job.

"I wonder what's happened." I speak aloud.

"I dread to think." Eve offers, staring off into space. I know she's had some bad things happen to her these past few months and, as I watch her, I know she's reliving some of those moments.

Within five minutes a not very happy looking Teresa joins us. She slumps down on the bench, crossing her arms over her pregnancy bump. "I can't believe they just did that!" She complains.

"What?" I ask.

"They ruined it! I seduced him and everything." She whines.

Eve laughs. "You don't need to seduce him, that man follows you around with his tongue hanging out, especially now you're at that stage of pregnancy where you're practically horny all the time."

I laugh because she's telling the truth. Both these women are so lucky that they have these men. Men who treat them with respect. Everyone can see how much they're loved, actually I think worshipped is a better word. Even Elle has Ink running around like a puppy after her. I just watch it all with a hint of jealousy. Don't get me wrong, I'm happy for them, but sometimes I just wish I could find someone like that for myself.

"But I needed him, he's been so busy with the club lately and I wanted some alone time. Angel just barged through the door and Bill went running off with him like I'm nothing."

Teresa's pregnancy has sent her hormones crazy. She's an emotional woman at the best of times, but now she's expecting it's on a whole other level.

Especially her sex drive, Teresa is sex mad these days.

The next one to join us in the yard is Elle and she plants herself beside me. "I can't believe I was just ignored!"

"Yeah I just saw Ink, he was right behind Angel when he stopped my sexy time. At least they didn't stop that." Teresa sulks.

"Sexy time?' Elle laughs. "I was just about to seduce him when he ignored me and went off to that bloody church room of theirs."

"Must be real serious." Eve looks at Teresa who nods her head in agreement.

"How do you know?" I ask.

Teresa looks to me. "This wasn't a planned church meeting, or Prez wouldn't have been with me, he knows I don't like having our time together cut short."

The loud growl of more bikes sound. We silently watch as more bikers I haven't seen before walk past us. Some of the bikers whistle and wink as they pass. When they disappear inside the clubhouse I ask who they were.

"They're from one of the partner charters." Eve answers.

"Which means we're right about it being serious." Teresa adds.

We decide to forget about the men and their meeting for now and have fun with Elizabeth.

About an hour later we hear a shout from the direction of the gates. I look to Elle. "Did you hear that?"

She nods, then we hear another shout, but this time it sounds like they're shouting for help. Teresa stands and we all move to follow. Eve looks to Teresa. "Stay here with Elizabeth."

Teresa uncharacteristically doesn't argue and pulls Elizabeth close as I follow Elle and Eve towards the gates. They're normally locked and have two prospects guarding them. They're ajar now and only one prospect is there, he's just ending a call on his phone as we arrive.

"What's happening?"

"It's Sue." He replies stone faced. "Something's wrong, she went out in her car a while ago, but she's just come back on foot and she collapsed outside. Jez has gone to bring her in."

"Sue!" Eve shouts, trying to break past him and get through the gate. He stops her.

"You've got to wait here miss, Angel would kill me if I let you out of here right now." He looks suitably apologetic at keeping Eve on this side of the gates.

"Sue?" Teresa shouts from the bench, having heard Eve's scream. "What's wrong?"

She starts to walk over but Elle shouts at her. "Stay where you are!"

Teresa pauses. I look on in shock as the prospect appears at the gate, Sue cradled in his arms. She looks terrified and is sobbing as she's carried in.

"Oh my god, Sue." Eve whispers.

"Get her inside quick." Elle yells as we all turn for the clubhouse. Jez follows us, Sue still secure in his arms as the other prospect rushes to lock the gate again.

Eve rushes ahead of us, screaming for Angel. As I run into the lounge room the church doors open

CARNAL PERSUASION (SEVERED MC #4)

and Angel comes running out. I spot Cowboy right behind him and shout at him.

"Cowboy!" Everyone turns to look at me like I'm insane. "It's Sue."

The church room quickly empties into the lounge, obviously hearing the panic in my voice. Doc moves for Sue as Angel asks Eve to get Elizabeth out of here The prospect who carried Sue in offers to take her into the playroom. Eve thanks him. As soon as Elizabeth is out of sight she rushes to Sue's side.

Angel and Prez are crouching down next to Sue. Prez speaks quietly. "Sue? What happened?"

"He came out of nowhere." She sobs.

"Who?" Ange asks.

Sue looks up at us all watching her and cries more loudly. Eve and Teresa sit down next to her to try and soothe her.

"I don't know, this strange man." She tries to calm her tears; her voice is shaking as much as she is. "I was in town and saw a lovely dress for Elizabeth that I just had to buy. When I made my way back to the car someone came at me from behind." She's rushing her words and tries to slow down as she continues. " I tried to cry out, but he covered my mouth, there was nobody around to help. He demanded money, then he took my car keys." She pauses as a huge sob racks her body. "He shoved me to the ground, then he kicked me in the stomach before taking my car."

During the whole exchange Sue has been holding her stomach in pain. "He took my purse." She sobs. "It's got my ring from Elvis in there." She really breaks down now.

Prez stands, looking pissed.

"We can get the CCTV Prez." Ink informs him.

"That would be perfect. Do it." Prez commands. Ink takes out his phone and walks into the next room. He then turns to Doc. "Get her to the hospital." Instantly Eve and Teresa move to go with them.

"I'll watch Elizabeth for you." I tell Eve.

"Thank you." She looks at me with tears in her eyes She loves Sue. I know she will want to go with Teresa.

On my way to the playroom, Cowboy stops me. "Stay here okay?"

"Why, are we in danger?" I ask, shocked at how this whole afternoon has changed for the worse.

He takes a deep breath and looks me over. "Just stay here, I need you to be safe while I'm at the hospital with the girls and Angel."

He kisses my forehead and then leaves me to go play with Elizabeth.

Another hour passes before I manage to put Elizabeth down for a nap. I'm about to step outside Angels and Eve's room to grab a quick drink when I overhear Ink and Prez talking outside. I stand there, the door ajar and listen in.

"It looked like an addict. Probably raising money for his next fix." Ink tells him.

"You're sure?" Prez asks.

"For sure. I know addicts; this one was the usual standard. My guess is he's connected to all the other crap the VP brought to the table."

"Shit." Prez curses. "We need to tell the others."

I hear them coming closer and quickly shut the door before they pass. What the fuck is going on around here?

Chapter Seven

Cowboy

Rabbit is the last to enter, closing the doors behind him. As soon as his ass hits the seat, Prez slams down the gavel to begin church meeting.

"Alright boys lets get straight to the point. I'm not in the mood for bullshit. Someone in Severed is dealing drugs right under our fucking noses. We're putting a stop to it!" He looks around us all, giving us his deathly stare. "This is not happening! We need to find these fuckers quickly before anyone else gets hurt."

The image of Sue being carried in by the Prospect enters my mind. In an instant Sue turns into Lucy. She's covered in blood, not making a sound. A shiver runs through me at the mental picture and I shake it off.

"Is Sue alright?" I ask, my voice still shaken from the pictures in my head.

"Eve called before I came to church." Angel answers. "She's doing okay, bruised ribs and hurt pride, but she's more upset about having Elvis's ring stolen from her."

Silence follows his words. We all know how important that ring is to Sue. She clings to it like a lifeline.

"Something needs to be done and quickly." Prez growls. "Someone's getting these dickheads too fucking high for their own good. Sue's already been hurt. I sure as shit don't want anyone else we love being put in harms way." He takes a deep breath. "We need to go down to the strip club and have a chat with the dancers to see if they know anything. Any volunteers?"

A number of hands rise. I can't help but laugh.

"What about you, Ink?" Prez asks him. Inks eyes widen.

"Erm, not to be disrespectful boss, but Elle would have my fucking balls if I stepped into that place. My dick too if she found out I'd volunteered for it."

There's laughter around the table. Prez asks Angel the same question. "VP? Fancy a trip?"

Angel laughs. "Same goes for me Prez. Eve wouldn't be happy."

Prez smile widens. "Well that's sorted then. Angel and Ink will be going to the strip club. Cowboy, Kid and Ice can go along with them. Time to show your women who's in control boys."

There's laughter again. I decide to remind Prez who his old lady is.

"You do know Teresa as well as we do, right?" I snicker.

"Yeah, Prez." Angel joins in. "How about you come along too? Show your old lady who's in charge?"

Prez's smile falls. "I ain't that fucking stupid, VP." Then he slaps Angel on his back and laughs along with the rest of us.

Prez slams his hands down on the table. "Right back to the matter in hand. You spoken to Scalp yet, Angel?"

"I got in touch with him, like we thought he said this isn't anything to do with them." Angel informs the room.

Prez nods his head thoughtfully. "Which means this is someone new."

"Or someone stupid enough to try." I add.

"Tell them what you found, Ink." Prez sounds tired. I'm not surprised, we all are.

"I talked to one of our contacts who owes us a favor, he managed to get us into the CCTV where Sue was attacked. The guy's definitely an addict; I tracked him on the tapes before and after he bumped into Sue. Looks like he was on the hunt for money to get his next fix."

"He hit the fucking jackpot when he saw our girl then." Angel grumbles.

We all love Sue, hurting her has pissed us all off. Not to mention hurt us. She means a lot to the whole club.

"Did you follow where he went?" Cherry asks.

"No." Ink shakes his head. "The CCTV was restricted, it wouldn't let me follow him all the way."

"We need to find Elvis's ring for her." Angel states.

"We will." Prez affirms. "I'll reach out to Scalp, I think we need to have a friendly sit down with him and his MC. This shit concerns us all. We may have had our troubles in the past," he pauses as we all remember just how bad things were, "we'll find these fuckers faster if we're working together."

Everyone nods their approval around the table.

"Right then. Off to the strip club boys and do some digging. We need to find out what those girls know."
Prez slams his gavel down, ending the meeting.

The room empties slowly; we're all dreading what's around the corner.

Chapter Eight

Eve

I really thought that I'd heard the last of the bike lessons after the other morning, but no. When I woke this morning Gabe decided I had to get dressed and go to the clubhouse with him as he has a surprise for me.

Judging by the shiny new, flat-heeled biker boots he just handed me, I'm guessing I'm in for yet more torture. Knowing what's ahead I decide to dress in my jeans, despite the heat of the day. I also go for a long sleeved t-shirt. I'm going to swelter in this outfit, but better safe than sorry. It's not like I'm under any illusion about how accident-prone I am.

When we get to the clubhouse Elizabeth runs straight in to find Teresa. She's fascinated by

Teresa's growing baby bump. She keeps asking us when she can have a baby brother or sister, but it's still too soon for us. The hurt of losing our baby hasn't gone away. I know it never will, but it's still too raw for me to think of trying again yet.

Gabe's like a child on Christmas morning the way he's carrying on. He's got a huge grin on his face. I dread to think what the surprise is. He takes my hand and drags me excitedly towards the bike shed. That's when I see it. Outside the shed, there's a shiny new red moped. It's glistening in the sun from its highly polished panels. It's pristine and obviously brand spanking new. Shit. This is not going to end well. I just have a sixth sense about it.

"Here you go, Princess." Gabe is beaming as he hands me the ignition key. It's in a black jewelers box, nestled on purple silk, with a ribbon tied around the outside. It's not quite what I was looking for in a jeweler's box I have to admit.

Plastering on a fake smile I pretend to be enthusiastic about my gift. "Oh Gabe, I love it, thank you so much." I gush, but he knows me too well; I can see the disappointment in his face.

"I thought you'd love it, baby. Something for you to get the hang of, then you can ride a proper bike." He kicks the dust at his feet. "Give it a go, you might love it." My heart drops as he loses the smile from his face. I'll never be the biker chick he wants me to be. I love the people, I really love Gabe, but I know my limitations and four wheels is the safest place for me to be when I'm the one in control.

I squeal in delight when I realize I can get the moped off the kickstand. Little things I know, but it makes me happy. From the smile back on Gabe's face I've made him happy too.

He's bought me what he calls a "twist and go'. There's no clutch to worry about, the levers on both handlebars are brakes. He goes through all the controls again. I'm only half listening as usual.

He frowns at me when I have to ask him to repeat what he just told me.

"Stop holding the brake and the throttle together." He admonishes. "Keep your hands away from the brakes until you need them."

"Okay boss." I smirk at him. This looks a lot easier than I was expecting. Gabe starts the bike up and asks me to take it slowly around the yard.

"It's not like a car Eve, you need to move your head so you're looking in the direction you want to go when you want to turn." That made no sense to me whatsoever, but I switch on the bike and set off along the yard slowly. And I mean *really* slowly. I'm lucky if I'm doing 10 mph here, but it sure as hell feels a lot faster.

For all it's solidity, the moped doesn't feel as stable as I thought it would. I advance up the yard, conscious that any second I'm likely to come crashing to the ground. In fact I'm going so slowly Gabe is able to walk at the side of me, offering words of encouragement as we go.

"That's it baby, give it a little more throttle now."

A couple of minutes later I'm told to do the opposite. "Ease off the throttle a little now, Eve. You need to think about turning." *Shit.* The lovely long yard has come to an end. I don't want to turn. Memories of being knocked off my bicycle when I was younger suddenly flash into my mind. That's not a good thought to have in your head as you're approaching a wall I can tell you.

"Turn your head!" Gabe shouts at me. I do as he says and I'm surprised when the bike seems to follow the direction I want to go in. I'm even more surprised when I realize I've turned the corner and am heading back in the other direction. I'm still feeling unstable on the bike, but I did it!

"Yay!" I shout out. That wasn't as bad as I expected.

"You can try and give it a little more throttle now," he tells me. I don't know that I want to do that. I'm more than happy with my sedate snails pace at the moment, but I give it a go just to keep him happy.

The rest of the morning passes with me squealing each time I master a new corner. Gabe even sets up some obstacles for me so I can practice pulling out at junctions and turning in. I'm feeling quite happy with it all, although I'm still not going any faster then 15mph in the compound.

"What do you say we take you out on the road for an hour, get some real practice?" Gabe suggests, looking a little too excited for my liking.

"What about Elizabeth?" Shit. The last place I want to be right now is out on a real road. I'm only just getting my confidence on this mini obstacle course he's created for me.

"She's with Teresa and she's fine." Gabe reassures me. "Give it a go. If you're not enjoying it, we'll turn round and come back." He offers. He gives me the puppy dog eyes he knows I can't resist and I'm done for.

"Okay, but you promise we can come back if I don't like it?" Gabe nods his head, then goes and gets his bike from the line up.

"You go first baby, I'll stay behind you and keep an eye on you. You can choose the route." He offers.

I pull my helmet back on, trying to give myself a talking to before we set off. I can do this. I can do this without falling off or making an absolute prat of myself. Yeah. Right. Maybe one day I'll believe that.

I head out of the compound, grateful that we're not closer to Severed, as the roads are a lot quieter round here. I panic when I hear a car coming up behind me and see one coming towards me, but the roads plenty wide enough for

CARNAL PERSUASION (SEVERED MC #4)

them to pass me. I settle my nerves a little and carry on.

We've probably been out an hour when I decide I've had enough, it means doing a uturn on the road as there's no where else to turn so I look over my shoulder to check for traffic. The road's clear so I indicate and start to turn.

And that's when it all goes horribly wrong. Don't ask me why, but instead of looking where I'm going I focus on the kerb on the other side of the road. Next thing I know I'm heading straight for it. Of course, I then panic and for some reason instead of braking, I throttle the moped and head towards it even faster. I'm not sure quite how it happens, but the next thing I know I'm lying on the road, flat on my back with the bike on top of me. Fuck, that thing is heavy, I can't move.

I turn my head to see Gabe rushing over to me. He looks deathly white when he gets to me and helps lift the bike off me. It might have been lighter than the motorbike the other day, but there's enough weight that I couldn't get up on my own.

"Shit, Eve. Are you okay? What happened? Where are you hurt?" He's firing the questions at me so fast I can't concentrate. His hands are touching everywhere they can, his eyes searching for any injury,

"Whoah!" I offer up. Now the bike is off me I can mentally survey the damage. I think I'm okay. The back of my thigh stings where it hit the road, but other than that I appear to be fine.

Gabe gives me his hand and helps me to my feet. I look at the bike he's holding and laugh. "Well, at least the bike's okay."

"Fuck the bike!" he growls. "Are you okay, Princess?"

I'm holding the back of my leg by now, but realize it's nothing more than a stinging sensation at the moment. "Yeah, I think my pride was hurt more than anything." I inspect the back of my jeans and am relieved there's no sign of tearing or damage. "I suspect I'll have a corker of a bruise later though." I laugh nervously.

"Shit baby, you scared the hell out of me." Gabe mutters. "That's it, no more bike lessons, only place you're going from now on is on the back of my bike." I'm so relieved to hear that I reach over and kiss him firmly on the lips.

Gabe gets his phone out and arranges for a couple of prospects to come out and pick up the moped, apparently he doesn't trust me to ride it back. I can't say I'm not pleased.

I throw a look of disdain at the shiny red machine as I jump on the back of Gabe's bike. I wrap my arms around him, snuggling in close. This is where I belong on a bike.

"Come on babe, let's get you home and check out those bruises." At least he's laughing about it now. I think I really scared him there for a moment.

As we pull into the yard at the clubhouse I don't think I've ever been so relieved to see it. Riding back was uncomfortable. I just know that when Gabe realizes I've probably bruised my ass, that I'll never hear the end of it.

Chapter Nine

Lucy

I knew Cowboy would give me a hard time when he found out I'd lost my job. I was right to keep it from him. He threatened to go to the office and deal with the 'lecherous old bastard' as he called him, on my behalf. It took me a good hour to calm him down.

Sometimes he's such an overprotective jerk. He acts like my big brother, although I've been comfortable with that for months, something changed the night he tried to kill himself. I can't seem to think of him like family now. God, the thoughts I have about him when I'm in bed on a night are definitely not the way you'd think of a family member. They're downright incestuous.

Once I'd managed to calm him down, the conversation then turned to my new job. I'm not sure which was worse.

"I don't fucking think so," he roared at me. "You are not working at that bar." He downright forbade me to go work at the bar.

That set my hackles on end. I detest being told what I can and can't do. I won't let him stop me though. I need this job. He doesn't know I've already started working there.

Tonight's the grand re-opening. I thought I'd be working, but it didn't take Declan long to realize I'd over exaggerated my experience and put me on day shifts only for the first few weeks. I think breaking half a dozen glasses on my training day might just have contributed to that. Still, I can't complain. I'm only doing the quiet shifts during the day. I won't get much in tips, but at least the basic salary will cover my rent. It also means I get to go on the girl's night out this evening. That's something else Cowboy told me I couldn't do. God, that man infuriates me sometimes.

After what happened to Sue the other day, all the guys have been hesitant about our night out. They won't come out and say it, but reading between the lines I think they suspect Declan of being involved in whatever shit is happening in Severed. They're wrong, I just know it. My gut tells me that even though I don't know him well, he's a good guy.

The compromise that we reached was that the girl's could have their night out, but that the guys would all be in attendance as well. Elle threatened them in her usual no nonsense way that they are to stay out of our way, unless we ask for their assistance. Part of the compromise was that I had to let Cowboy give me a lift there and back.

The atmosphere between us is a little frosty at the moment. When he sees what I plan on wearing tonight, I'm pretty sure that all hell will break out.

Eve may have to wear a long skirt, thanks to some accident she's a bit reluctant to discuss, but I don't. I look at the tiny leather look skirt hanging on the closet door. I'm not sure if I've got the balls to wear it if I'm truthful. It's the shortest thing I've ever owned. I own sweater dresses longer than that, but even those I wear with leggings or jeans.

Balls to it! I've got great legs. I see no reason why I shouldn't show them off for a change. I'm sure if Emma was here she'd be encouraging me to go for it. I pull out my most comfortable shiny, black stilettos and together with a fake leather black collared corset my outfit is complete. I stand back and look at my reflection in the full length mirror I normally try and avoid. I think it looks good, but just to be safe, I take a selfie and send it to Elle. Her reply comes back moments later.

ELLE: You look hot, tart!

That'll do for me. A huge grin breaks out on my face. I'm really looking forward to this night out. I'll miss Emma, but over the last few months the girls at Severed MC have taken me under their wing and made me feel like I'm part of them. I'm not sure if Holly will come tonight. She's still struggling with her grief over losing both her brother and best friend. She has good days, but she has more bad days. It would be good to get her out and have her let her hair down. We all need it. We haven't had a girls night out since before Justice died.

A frown crosses my face at the memory of that night. It's the first time I met Cowboy. He was drunk and miserable, but it didn't stop him coming to my defense when some guy got all handsy on me.

I apply the finishing touches to my make up. I don't normally wear much, just a hint of blush, a subtle eye color and some pale lipstick. I notice a lipstick sitting untouched in my make up drawer. It's one that Emma bought for me, she told me I needed to try bolder colors and handed over this dark red one. I've never worn it. I peel off the cellophane wrapper and stare at the opened lipstick. I'm already well out of my comfort zone with my outfit, but why the hell not. I'm tired of being quiet little Lucy. It's time I stood up for myself and showed off the figure I spend too much time hiding under baggy clothes. With the vivid lipstick in place I don't recognize the girl staring back at me from the mirror. She looks like a stranger. A sexy stranger at that. Oh well, do or die as they say.

Cowboy has his back to me when I enter the living room. he's watching some American show about custom bikes. The click of my heels on the hardwood floor alerts him to my presence. He almost chokes when he sees me. The way he does a double take is almost comical. I'd have laughed at the expression on his face, if only he didn't have such a dark, sour look on his face. I knew he'd overreact.

"You can go get changed right fucking now, " he splutters, "You are not leaving this house dressed like that."

"What the fuck?" I blurt out. "Who do you think you are? My bloody father?" I'm furious. I'm also sick to the back teeth of this guy trying to control my life. "I'll wear what the fuck I want. No one tells me what I can or can't do, so go back into your fucking cave you Neanderthal."

Cowboy actually looks shocked at my outburst. We've had disagreements before, but I've never fought back this loudly or vocally. I've always been quite calm, but firm in my responses. It only takes him a moment to recover though.

"I am not taking you out in that outfit so go get changed, now!" He commands.

"Number one, you're not taking me out, you're just giving me a lift." I count off my imaginary checklist on my fingers. "Number two, I'll wear what the fuck I want. If that's a problem for you then get out of my house and leave me be. I can quite happily walk there." Okay, that last bit might be an exaggeration. There's no way I can walk all the way to the bar in these shoes, they'll be crippling my feet just from an evening of dancing as it is, but there's no way I'm backing down.

"You can't go on the back of the bike like that. You'll have to change." He huffs. He thinks he's won.

"I have no intention of going on the back of your bloody bike. You mean to tell me you didn't bring the truck? I'm definitely walking then." He can't seriously have thought I'd be going on the back of his bike on a girl's night out?

"What's wrong with my bike?" He shouts, clearly offended now.

"Do I really need to explain?" I ask him. He just stands there looking both confused and angry. "I'm going dancing. There's no way I'm going dancing in an outfit that I'd need to wear to go on the back of your bike." I huff. He still doesn't answer me so I throw my hands up in the air. "For Gods sake, what is your problem?"

"You look like a fucking tart." Cowboy blurts out, instantly going quiet as soon as the words have left his mouth and rightly so. I've never been so insulted in my life. The corset is actually sitting quite high on my bust. You can't see my ass cheeks in the skirt, it's short, but not that short. It's a great outfit for a night out. I've taken care to make sure I don't look like a club whore.

"Get out of my house, now." I hiss quietly. "Don't ever come back." I turn and walk back into my bedroom, slamming the door so hard the whole wall vibrates.

I sit down on the bed heavily. I gulp in deep, calming breaths. I will not cry. I'm determined not to give him the satisfaction of knowing how much he's hurt me with his words.

A few minutes later there's a gentle tap on the door. I hear Cowboy's hesitant voice. "Lucy, I'm sorry babe. I didn't mean that."

"But you said it." I'm quiet, but firm in my reply.

The door opens a crack. Cowboy sticks his head into the room. "I'm sorry. I shouldn't have said it. You took me by surprise. Can I come in? Please?" he pleads. His face looks full of remorse so I motion to the bed at the side of me with my head. Cowboy slinks his way across the room. The bed dips as his weight hits the mattress.

"I'm sorry. I just... I've never seen you look like that before.'

I give him a questioning look.

"What I mean is... Fuck... well, you look hot as fuck in this get up and I don't think I can handle all those fuckers ogling you in the bar all night long." I feel my cheeks burn at the honesty in his words.

Cowboy has never once told me he thinks of me in that way, I must be misunderstanding him.

"Look, I'm young, free and single. I'll wear what I want, when I want. I'll work where I bloody well want as well." I face him. "You don't have any right to dictate any of that shit to me. Get it?" My voice might sound firm, but inside I'm a bag of nerves. "You're not my father Cowboy and you sure as hell ain't my boyfriend." I stand quickly to exit the room on my now shaky legs.

I'm not sure if I imagine his parting words, but I'd swear he said he wished he was my boyfriend as I slammed the door behind me.

Chapter Ten

Lucy

Cowboy's been pretty quiet since our row. He followed me into the living room and told me that if I'd give him half an hour he'd go swap his bike for the truck. He didn't want me out there on my own at the moment. He didn't need to remind me about what happened to Sue, but I could tell that's what he was thinking of.

The drive to the bar was in silence, save for the radio in the truck. I couldn't tell you what was playing as my mind was too distracted by what I thought I'd heard him say as I left my bedroom. I must have misheard him. There's no way Cowboy would want a quiet little mouse like me as a girlfriend.

The bar looks to be heaving as we pull up, granted it's a grand re-opening and drinks are half price tonight so that may have something to do with it. When we walk through the door I can physically feel the heat and energy that the place is giving off. Cowboy guides me to the bar, his hand protectively on my back the whole way. He orders our drinks while I scan the crowded room for our friends.

"Lucy!" I hear a drunken screech. It's Elle. A smile breaks out on my face as she rushes over to greet me. I love Elle; she's probably the most outspoken of the girls and a real rebel. I wish I could be more like her. She always looks amazing. She has this air of confidence about her. She snatches my drink from Cowboy and drags me over to a table that looks to be as far away from the guys as they could get. Cowboy just shrugs his shoulders and heads over to join the guys.

When I reach the girl's table I see that Holly is out so I greet her with a warm hug. It's so good to see her. Even Teresa has joined us, although as I arrive she's complaining about being stuck on soft drinks and looking like a beached whale. That girl always seems to be whining about something. I spot Eve rolling her eyes at Teresa as I greet Diane.

"Where's Sue?" I ask.

"She's babysitting for me," Eve offers.

"How is she?" I ask as I sit down next to her.

"She's doing okay, but she's staying with us for a few days. She wanted somewhere quiet to recuperate." I nod my head in understanding. I can understand her wanting to avoid busy places for a while.

"Holy fuck! Who's that?" Elle exclaims rather loudly. I look up from my drink to see Declan walking towards us.

"That my dear is my new boss." I tell her.

"No fucking way. That man is hot with a capital H." She blurts out. We all laugh at her. She's right. Declan looks hot in his low hung jeans and tightly fitted white shirt. From the number of admiring glances he gets as he makes his way to our table, we're not the only ones to notice.

"How's my favorite barmaid doing?" Declan greets me with a kiss on the cheek.

"Fine boss, thanks." Oops. Across the room I can tell Cowboy saw the kiss and has the biggest scowl on his face. What's his problem? Thankfully Angel has a restraining hold on his arm.

"Let me introduce you to my friends." I go around the table introducing each of the girls, who all flirt with him outrageously, then I get to Holly. Declan's attention is firmly fixed on her. It looks like the attraction is mutual from the blush rising up Holly's neck. Who'd have guessed? I'll have to see if I can't breathe some life into that pair. It's about time something good happened for Holly.

Declan calls one of the bar staff over to take our order and offers us drinks on the house for the rest of the evening. The girls decide that we're doing a round of shots. I groan inwardly at the anticipation of the hangover I'm going to have in the morning. I'm not good with hangovers.

"I'll leave you charming ladies to your evening and go attend to the rest of my guests." He bows low as he leaves causing Elle to splutter into her glass of wine. I don't miss the way his eyes linger on Holly before he turns to leave.

"Fuck me. You work with him?" She queries. "How the fuck do you keep your hands off him?"

The girls around the table look at me expectantly. "He's my boss, that's all." I offer.

Declan's hot yes, he's also very charming, but I can't say I think of him that way. Instead I find my head turning to seek out Cowboy who's glaring at our table. My smile in his direction only softens his features slightly. Angel, Prez and Ink don't look overly happy right now either. Looks like this could be an interesting evening.

**

Cowboy

Angel has to physically hold me back when that fucker kisses Lucy on the cheek. "What's wrong with you?" he asks.

"Nothing." I grumble in response. Truth be told, I don't know what's wrong with me. Ever since I saw Lucy walk out of her bedroom in that fucking short skirt I've been sporting a hard on. The fact she argued back just made it worse. I love a strong woman. Lucy showed tonight she's got a real inner strength. I want nothing more than to march over there and drag her away from the prying eyes of the other men in here.

Angel is looking at me with suspicion in his eyes. "There something going on between you and Lucy?"

CARNAL PERSUASION (SEVERED MC #4)

"Nothing." I repeat, maybe a little too quickly.

"Do you want there to be?" He asks with that knowing smirk of his.

"Of course not." I bluster. No sooner have the words left my mouth than I question myself. Do I? My feelings for Lucy have changed; even I've noticed that. I no longer look at her as a little sister I need to protect that's for sure. I still want to care for her, but on a whole other level.

"Really?" Ink joins in. "Doesn't look that way from where I'm sitting brother."

"I'm no good for her. She deserves better than me." I reply sullenly.

"What a fucking load of bollocks." Prez joins in. "She'd be lucky to have you." I look at him in surprise. "Lucy's a nice girl, she needs someone like you to take care of her." He finishes.

I stare at the beer bottle in my hand. "I can't take care of anyone." I mutter. "Look at all the people I've let down over the past few months." I can't look up at them.

"What a load of complete bollocks." Angel snaps. That gets my attention. "You've been through some terrible shit this year, we all have," he states, "but I would always trust you to have my back, or to protect my family." He looks over at Eve as he says the last words.

"Same here." Ink and Prez say at the same time.

I look at my friends in shock. They really feel that way about me? I thought they'd think I was a total failure.

"You don't seriously believe that crap you just spouted do you?" Angel sounds concerned. I don't say anything; I can't say anything right now. "Fuck! You do." He shakes his head in exasperation. "Why didn't you tell me? I'm your friend, or I thought I was." He sounds disappointed.

"We re all your friends." Ink says.

"Fuck, yes." Prez adds. "You're part of us, Cowboy. We're a fucking family."

Emotion threatens to get the better of me, so I stand quickly to hide it.

"Enough of this girly shit," I announce. "Who wants another drink?". Thankfully the guys let it go and give me their drink orders. They don't mention it again the rest of the evening.

The main reason we're here this evening is to keep a watchful eye on our women, but in between we're all scanning the bar for anything out of place. We're suspicious of this Declan guy. No one seems to know anything about his past; even Lucy couldn't tell me anything when I told her she wasn't working here. It's too much of a coincidence that he rides into town and we suddenly have a drug problem in Severed.

The girls seem to be having a great time, granted. a little worse for wear. No one bothers them, but then most people in Severed know who the girls are with.

The DJ announces the last song of the evening and the girls let out a loud groan from the dance floor. Angel, Ink and Prez take that as their cue to go have a slow dance with their women. Lucy looks around expectantly, but seeing me still seated at the table shrugs her shoulders and leaves the dance floor to go sit with Diane.

There's a chorus of 'Good night's" and "Love you's" as we escort the girls from the pub into the well lit car park at the back. Lucy is definitely the worse for wear as she stumbles along on her heels, before swearing loudly and making a show of taking them off. The stupid girl's planning on walking the rest of the way to the truck barefoot. Fuck that. There's still some building rubble on the ground from the refit so I scoop her up into my arms. She's so wasted she just leans her head against my shoulder, sighing lightly against my chest.

I fasten her into the truck and she falls asleep as soon as her head hits the backrest. She looks so at peace when she's sleeping. She's still out of it when I pull up at her apartment. I search through her bag for her keys and then scoop her up in my arms again. It's a little awkward trying to open her front door whilst still holding her, but I get there eventually.

I walk through to her bedroom and lay her gently on the bed. I'm not sure what to do. She can't be comfortable sleeping in that outfit, but I don't know if I should undress her or not. She would understand, wouldn't she? I decide to remove the skirt and top for her. "Fuck." I curse under my breath. That was a mistake. Lucy's laid there, in skimpy underwear that showcases the hot figure she normally hides. My dick stands to attention, protesting at being restrained in my jeans.

I lift the blanket from the chair at the side of her bed and cover her carefully with it. The hardest thing I've ever done is to walk out of that room and leave her there on her own. I contemplate staying on the sofa, but I know myself. I wouldn't be able to stay on the sofa after seeing her like that.

I close the door quietly behind me on my way out, testing that it's locked and I head back to the clubhouse. I'm in desperate need of a cold shower.

Chapter Eleven

Eve

Gabe cuts the engine as we pull up in front of our house and helps me off the bike. I can't do it myself, as the long skirt I had to wear would make me fall on my ass. I had to wear it though; the bruising on the back of my leg is really bad. It's fifty shades of bruised - all blacks, blues and yellows, I don't want anyone seeing that, not even Gabe, although he insists on getting me naked any chance he can get.

Gabe swoops me up into his arms before gently placing me back on my feet. He doesn't take his eyes off me, his blue eyes staring into mine. He still takes my breath away, even after all this time together. His eyes devour me and I can't look away. A chill sends a shock right through me and

Gabe grins in that smug way he has. He's knows exactly what he's doing to me.

"You are so fucking gorgeous, Princess." He growls. I don't have time to respond before his mouth is on mine. Gabe kisses me like his life depends on it. I melt into him, gripping his body anywhere I can until my hands find his dirty blonde locks and pull hard. Gabe moans in return and I smile against his mouth. That is until he slaps my ass in a playful way, something he always loves to do. Normally I'd love it, but right now I have a huge bruise decorating my ass and I gasp. Realizing what he's done Gabe lets me go.

"Shit, babe! I forgot, sorry."

I rub my ass as the pain lessens; when I look back to Gabe he has a smile on his face. "Are you laughing at me?"

His grin widens and is followed by laughter. "Oh baby, it's just so fucking funny. Now that I know you're okay, I can see the funny side."

I frown at him. "Yeah, well my ass doesn't think so."

Gabe makes fun of me by poking out his bottom lip. "I love your ass, even though you now have three ass cheeks instead of two." He laughs. "There's more to play with." He's right; the swelling on the back of my leg does make it look like I have an extra ass cheek.

I slap him across his chest. "Be careful Gabe, you won't be getting any more of this ass if you carry on."

Gabe stops laughing, but his smirk is still in place. "Don't threaten me baby, you know I love this body of yours." He kisses me again. "You know I can't help myself when you call me by my real name."

I try to push him away. "Then don't make fun of me."

Gabe holds me in place, still smiling. "You're so fucking adorable when you sulk."

I open my mouth wide in shock. "I am not sulking!"

I almost stomp my foot in frustration, then am glad I didn't because it would only have proved him right."

Gabe leans in close again and kisses me. I try not to give into him, but his kisses are so damn good I can't help it. I moan against his lips, aligning myself as close as possible to his hard body. God, I need him now!

Gabe grabs my ass and squeezes which causes me to yelp. "Ouch!"

Gabe places his finger over my mouth, thankfully letting go of my ass. "Be quiet woman, you'll wake up Elizabeth and Sue."

Gabe rests his forehead against mine. "God, it's like living with my parents." He complains.

I laugh, it's a little louder than I would like, probably a result of all that alcohol I consumed back at the bar.

Gabe presses his hardened cock against me. "God, I want you so fucking bad baby girl."

I almost laugh at this. Gabe's a man who likes to make love to me hard; I love it just as much. With Sue living with us at the moment he won't be able to have me the way he craves.

Gabe backs me up so I'm pressed against the house and kisses me into a frenzy. He almost makes me dizzy with his talented mouth. Lifting up my left leg he thrusts against me again, his hard cock pressing into me. I groan as I feel him through the thin material of my skirt.

"Gabe," I break away from his lips. "I can't do this out here."

I look around in the darkness, anybody could be watching. The thought of it gives me the creeps.

Gabe groans. "But I want you baby, I want to sink my cock into you as deep as I can. I want to hear you screaming."

He looks me up and down before taking my hand. "Gabe, what are you doing?"

He leads me around the side of the house to where his garage is. "Finding us some privacy."

When Gabe isn't on club business or at the clubhouse, he can normally be found out in his garage fixing up any old thing. He stops in front of it and unlocks the door. As soon as he's ushered me inside he's all over me. His kisses trail down my neck, when my top stops him he pulls it off over my head. He quickly removes my bra and gives my nipples some much-deserved attention. I gasp at the sensation. God, I love his mouth on my breasts. I claw at his leather cut and shirt.

"Take them off." I beg him. "I need to feel you."

He lets me go in order to strip. As I watch him undress I let my skirt float to the floor, removing my thong. We stand staring at each other for just a minute, taking in each other's glorious naked bodies. Gabe reaches for his rock hard cock, teasing me.

I watch him as he walks over to a chair hidden amongst bikes and spare parts. He sits down, his dick in his hand. "Come over here baby." He gestures for me to come to him.

I slowly make my way over. When I reach him he places his hands on my waist, careful not to touch any bruises. "Ride me." He commands.

"On that chair?" I smile. It doesn't look like it can take the weight of both of us.

"Sit on my lap and ride me." He tells me again, all playfulness gone.

I lift my leg over him, as I'm about to straddle him he grabs my leg and halts it in mid-air. "Look at that."

He looks directly at my core, exposed to his eyes. He groans deep in his chest before starting to rub his finger back and forth. My head tilts back and I moan.

"You like that baby?" Gabe asks.

"Yes." I whisper.

Gabe stops his fingering and helps settle my leg down so that I'm straddling him. I can feel his deliciously hard cock against my wetness. I start to grind against it, the friction is amazing. Gabe lifts me, before slamming me down onto his cock. My eyes roll from the pleasure, then my vision goes black.

"Oh my God!" I scream.

I automatically grind against him. Gabe's hands on my waist help me to take him faster and deeper. The bruise on my leg stings, but I can handle the pain. It's nothing compared to the feeling of Gabe buried deep inside me.

I whimper as he toys with my clit with his thumb. "Come for me." He growls.

I bite down on my lip as I let the pleasure take over. Gabe quickly finds his own release. I lay down against him, our sweaty bodies sticking together, but I don't care. I just want to be close to him. Gabe softly tickles my back with his fingertips as I gather my breath back.

"We'd better get inside." Gabe suggests quietly.

I open my eyes and realize I was almost falling asleep. Gabe helps me to slowly get off his lap. I try and locate my thong. Putting it back on I decide to wear Gabe's white shirt instead of mine. Giggling like children, we run back to the house, the rest of our clothes gathered in our hands and sneak to our bedroom as quietly as possible.

I head to the bathroom to clean myself up, before making my way to the bed, where Gabe is waiting for me. He lifts the cover for me and I snuggle in close, loving his warmth.

"Love you, Princess." He kisses my forehead.

"Love you." I whisper back.

Chapter Twelve

Lucy

When I wake the first thing I can feel is my pounding head, then I notice my dry mouth. I hate hangovers. I'm mortified when I realize that under the blanket I'm only wearing my underwear. I struggle to find my last conscious memory, but can't seem to focus on anything beyond the car park at the pub last night. I think I remember Cowboy carrying me to his truck when I took my shoes off. At that thought my eyes widen and a flush creeps over my cheeks.

He wouldn't have, would he?

The thought of Cowboy putting me to bed and stripping me down to my underwear has me blushing with shame. I've fantasized about him seeing me in my lingerie, but that involved me being compos mentis at the time. I cringe, hoping that I didn't do anything more embarrassing than passing out on him. Please God, let me not have told him I fancy him, or have asked him to do anything of the things I dream about him doing to me.

Gingerly I raise my head from the pillow, but lay it down again with a groan. *What did I drink last night?* My head feels like someone's smashing their way out with a sledgehammer and my stomach is so queasy that I'm pretty sure I'm going to throw up if I try and eat anything.

Looking at the clock on the nightstand I'm horrified to see that it's already eleven thirty in the morning. Shit. I was supposed to be at work at eleven. I've not even had my job a week and I'm already letting my new boss down.

I scan the room for my handbag, hoping that Cowboy remembered to bring it in with him. There's no sign of it, but I do see my clothes neatly folded on the chair at the side of the bed.

Sitting on top of them is my mobile phone, plugged into the charger I keep there. I make a mental note to thank Cowboy, assuming I can ever get over my embarrassment and speak to him again.

I reach for the phone, but have to wait several minutes for my eyes to actually focus on the small screen. The words all blur into each other for far too long. That's it, I'm never drinking like that again I vow Yeah, right. There's no way I can go on a night out with the girls and stay sober.

When my eyes finally decide to focus I see I have several missed calls and voice messages. Most of them are from Cowboy, which I quickly skip over, jumping to the voice mail from my new boss, Declan.

"Hi, Lucy. Cowboy rang to say you were under the weather today and wouldn't be able to make your shift. I've swapped it with Chas and you're now working Sunday lunch instead. Give me a call when you're feeling better to let me know you got my message." Shit. I delete the message, sighing loudly. What the hell was Cowboy thinking interfering with my job? I'd ring him right now and give him a piece of my mind, if I didn't feel quite so ill.

I look at the calls I've missed from Cowboy and see that he's been ringing every fifteen minutes for the last few hours. I'm not sure my head can handle the verbal lashing I'm sure he's left for me, but I press play on the voicemail and hope it's not as bad as I feared.

The first few messages are brief. Cowboy's just checking up on me, to make sure I'm okay. The more I listen to the messages, the more anxious they become. In one he lets me know he's spoken to Declan and switched my shift for me. At no point does he reference the state I must have been in last night. I'm beyond grateful for that. Then I get to his last message.

Shit. Cowboy doesn't sound very happy. "Lucy, for fucks sake, I'm sick of you ignoring me. I'm on my way over now." I check the time in a panic, that message was sent half an hour ago. Sure enough, just as the message has finished playing there's a banging on the front door.

I contemplate ignoring it and hiding my head under the pillow, but as the banging becomes more persistent I remind myself that this is Cowboy and he isn't going to go away.

Gingerly I lift myself from the bed, wrap my thin dressing gown around me and head for the front door. He's mid knock when I open the door. I've caught him by surprise and he almost lands on me as he starts to fall forward.

I can tell by the look on his face he's about to lay into me, but I must look worse than I feel as his expression suddenly softens.

"Well look what the cat dragged in," he chuckles. "You finally decided to rejoin the land of the living then?" I want to smack the smug bastard, but right now I need to sit down more.

I manage a quick glare before turning my back on him. I walk over to the sofa where I gratefully crash down and sink into the cushions. I close my eyes to try and stop my head spinning. The sound of Cowboy slamming the front door causes me to wince. I hear his heavy boots making their way over to me.

Cowboy is still laughing when he slumps down beside me. I manage to peer at him through one eye and catch him looking me over appraisingly.

"Look at the state of you woman." He mutters. "You had anything to eat yet?"

I shake my head in response, then groan as I feel the effects of the movement. Cowboy stands and makes his way over to the kitchen counter, muttering about women not being able to handle their drink. He pours me a glass of water and searches in the drawers for some painkillers.

"Make yourself at home why don't you?" I grumble.

"Shut up and take these," he demands, handing me the glass and the pills. I swallow the pills down with a mouthful of the blissfully cold water and sink further back into the cushions of the sofa.

"I'm dying." I moan.

"No you're not, you're just hung-over is all." His eyes show the laughter he's trying not to release. I could lose myself in those deep, dark eyes. They're hypnotizing. "Earth to Lucy." Cowboy interrupts me. From the questioning look he's giving me I've obviously missed something.

"Eh? What?' I mumble.

"I see you're still not with us." He chuckles. He sits down next to me again, this time drawing me into him. I'm too tired to complain and, truth be told, I like being in his arms. He makes a bloody good cushion, rock hard abs and all. There's something comforting about sitting close with him like this. Why can't he be more like this all the time instead of the Neanderthal?

I wake with a start to find I'd fallen asleep on Cowboy's chest. Shit, I even drooled on his shirt! I must have been well out of it. I quickly wipe my mouth, then the saliva from his top. I almost die when I see the wet patch I've created. He looks down on me and instead of the mocking I expected, it's compassion that I see in his eyes.

"Back with us then?" he smirks at me.

"What time is it?" I look around blindly for any evidence of the time.

"It's after three. You passed out on me, again." Oh shit. I can't believe I've just slept on him for several hours.

"I'm so sorry." I mumble in response.

"No need. You obviously needed it. My shirt will dry." He smirks, making no effort to move me, so I stay where I am. I'm too comfortable to move right now. The pills have obviously kicked in as the banging in my head has receded.

"Err. Last night…" I pause, unsure how to phrase my question.

"You passed out on me in the car park and I brought you home." Cowboy offers.

"And?" I question. I really wish I could remember more.

"And nothing. What do you take me for?" His voice deepens as a scowl appears on his face. Shit. I've offended him now.

"I didn't mean anything by it." I whisper. "I just don't remember getting undressed is all."

"You didn't." He grins at me now. It's a lascivious grin that's for sure. "I undressed you."

"Oh." I blush madly.

"Can't complain," he continues. "I quite enjoyed the view." Shit. Now I blush even more madly than before.

"Look..." We both say at the same time. Could this be anymore uncomfortable? I gesture for him to continue.

Cowboy smiles, but to my surprise he also looks a little nervous. "Look, Lucy. I'll be honest with you. I think you're fucking gorgeous. You're something else and we get on great. Don't get me wrong, I'd love to have you in my bed, but you're too good for me. You need a decent bloke in your life. Someone who'll look after you and give you what you need, not some broken biker." Cowboy hangs his head at the last words.

It hurts me to see him like this. I reach over and lift his chin with my finger to bring him eye level with me. "Don't you ever put yourself down like that again." I don't recognize the firm voice I'm using on him, but his words have made me angry. "You *are* a decent bloke. You're one of the nicest guys I know." I stop myself before adding he's also one of the most beautiful men I know. I don't think a tattooed biker would appreciate being called beautiful.

He looks at me expectantly. I'm unsure how to continue. Do I dare tell him how I feel? Will it ruin our friendship? As much as I want to have more with Cowboy, I don't want to lose our friendship, it means too much to me. I take a deep breath before I continue.

"What if I don't want a decent bloke, what if I want you?" I ask him "I'd love to be in your bed." I add on a whisper.

I've obviously said the wrong thing as he suddenly pushes me aside and stands. He paces back and forth over the small living room area, raking his hands through his short dark hair. I hang my head, shame coursing through me. I should have kept quiet.

I sense him in front of me. This time it's Cowboy who lifts my face to his. Looking into my eyes he gives me a glimmer of hope. "Lucy, I want you so fucking badly, but I can't do that to you. You deserve a relationship; you should be wined and dined. I'm not that guy." He looks crestfallen. Fuck, if I'm honest with myself, I'm disappointed too.

A frown appears on his face. "The idea of anyone else having you tears me apart. I don't know what to do, Lucy." He sounds in pain, but to me it's so simple.

"How about we try?" I ask. He looks shocked. "Just test the waters, see if we get on. If you don't think it's right, then end it."

Cowboy looks at me. "Lucy, baby, it won't be me ending it, it would be you. I'm the damaged one. You're so innocent." He pauses. "The thought of hurting you scares me." He continues to look at me. I guess he's processing what we've just said.

"Ah fuck it.' He suddenly exclaims. "Let's do it." I look at him, disbelief on my face. Did he say what I think he just said?

"What?"

"Let's try it and see if we can make a go of this." His smile is back now. "I'll pick you up at seven and take you out for a meal." He looks pleased with himself. He's just told me we're going out, he didn't ask. The control freak in me wants to tell him to go to hell, but I can't. I want to see if this works as well.

"It's a date." I smile up at him. He grins back at me, then turns and heads for the front door. What the hell? "You're going?" I blurt out.

"Yep, back at seven babe." And with that he's gone. The whole thing was so surreal I'm not sure it even happened. I pinch myself, then squeal when I feel the pain. Yep, that was real all right. I'd better go start getting ready.

Chapter Thirteen

Lucy

Getting out of the hot bath I feel sick. Wrapping the towel securely around me I crash onto the sofa. My heart is beating so fast in my chest it feels as though my whole body is vibrating. Surely this can't be nerves about the evening ahead.

It takes me a good while for my racing heart to calm down. I am so nervous. I don't know why, this is Cowboy. I know him, I adore him and God, yes, I fancy the hell out of him. Maybe that's the problem. I've built my hopes so high they can only be dashed. You only have to look at Cowboy, he's gorgeous. And me? I'm just me.

I haven't got much time before he'll be here. As he hasn't told me where we're going for dinner I'm unsure what to wear. In the end I choose what I think is a safe option. It's a floaty summer dress. It's long enough to graze the top of my knees and only hints at my cleavage so should meet his expectations. I shudder at the memory of him telling me to change last night.

I add minimal makeup this evening, a touch of blush and a hint of lip-gloss. I brush my long hair, leaving it loose on my shoulders, before slipping into some comfortable heels. Checking my reflection in the mirror I'm happy with the look. It's a very different look from last night.

I'm ready a little earlier than I expected and the wait is almost unbearable. I sit primly on the sofa so as not to crease my dress. When I'm not twiddling my thumbs I'm flicking through the channels on the TV, unable to concentrate.

There's a knock at the door and I get up to answer it, my heart beating from my chest again.

***

Cowboy

Lucy answers the door, her face a little paler than normal. I hope she's okay. Perhaps I shouldn't have suggested a meal out tonight when she's still recovering from last night. I didn't want to waste any time though. The thought of her being with anyone else fucking kills me. As much as I know she can do better, I don't want her to. I want her to be mine.

She looks amazing in a floral, waffy dress that showcases her waist and just hints at her breasts. Fuck. I've got a hard on already just looking at those legs of hers in heels.

"Hey." She greets me shyly. Where's my little hellcat gone?

"You look beautiful." I tell her, leaning in to give her a kiss on her cheek. She blushes again. What the fuck?

"Thank you. Shall we go?" she grabs her clutch from the table at the side of the door and before I know it she's outside with me, the door locked behind her. "Where are we going?" She asks expectantly.

"The Italiar" I offer. All chicks love Italian food don't they? I figured it was a fairly safe bet.

"Lovely." She looks nervous. Is she scared of me? Did she not want to go out? She cautiously reaches her hand out and takes hold of mine. I guess I'm just overreacting after all. Her small hand fits so perfectly in mine, it feels like she was made just for me. I shrug off the sentimentality and head us towards my bike.

"Oh." She sounds disappointed. "I wasn't expecting the bike. Can we walk? It's not far."

"What's wrong with the bike?" I ask, offended.

"Nothing." She's quick to reply. "I just wasn't expecting it so I'm not dressed for it." She sounds hurt now. Fuck. Why all of a sudden do we seem to have lost the ability to talk to each other?

I reluctantly agree to walk, she's right, it's not that far from here, but vow that I'll get her on the back of my bike before too long. That's where she belongs.

The Italian is noisy and crowded when we enter. There's some stag party going on and I groan when we're seated at the table next to them. The waiter apologizes that it's the only table they have left. I'm about to complain when Lucy places a restraining hand on my arm and smiling sweetly tells him that this will be fine.

I don't want to upset her so agree. I'm starting to get pissed with the attention the waiter is showing Lucy, pulling out her chair for her, almost placing the napkin in her lap until I snatch it from his hand. "We're fine now thank you." Lucy gives me a warning look. I try and rein it in a bit for her sake.

The evening doesn't go well. It's hard to relax and enjoy myself when I'm so distracted by the stag party leering at Lucy. I only offer monosyllabic answers in response to her questions. She looks relieved when the food arrives which leaves me feeling like shit.

The food is gorgeous, I've almost finished my meal but Lucy is toying with hers.

"What's up babe?" I dare to ask her.

She assures me there's nothing wrong with it. One of the guys from the stag party falls onto Lucy as he tries to return to his seat. That's when I lose it. Standing so quickly the table almost topples I end up spilling Lucy's meal on her lap. I hear her gasp, but I don't take my eyes from the dickhead in front of me. I'm so intent on smashing my fist into his face that nothing else matters right now.

I'm stopped when I hear Lucy screaming my name. The guy I was about to hit slinks off to his seat, as far away from me as he can get. Fucking coward. Lucy stands in front of me, tears in her eyes and pasta sauce running down the skirt of her dress. Oh fuck.

"You can't behave like this!" She screams at me. "You're so bloody jealous and possessive it's scary." There's a cold anger in her words.

"I'm not." I pout. Lucy then proceeds to remind me about the waiter, the several comments I've made to the stag party table whenever any of them looked in her direction and my comments about her outfit last night. Shit. I've really riled her up here.

"This was supposed to be our first date. Look at how it's gone." I cant bare to hear the hurt in her voice.

Lucy slams her napkin down on the table when I almost punch out the waiter who's come back and is trying to sponge down her skirt for her. "That's it." She screams. "I'm out of here."

CARNAL PERSUASION (SEVERED MC #4)

Before I can think, she's gone, the front door of the restaurant slamming behind her. There's a nervous giggle from the stag party table. I turn a deathly glare to the culprit who silences it quickly. The only reason I haven't ended these pricks yet just walked out the door.

All eyes in the restaurant are on me. Fuck. See, I knew I couldn't do this relationship crap.

"Follow her." A quiet female voice whispers into my ear. I turn to see a young waitress standing at my side. "Follow her quickly. You need to go and apologize." She advises. She wants me to fucking apologize? I did nothing wrong. I'm about to protest when she silences me. "Trust me." Is all she says. Fuck it. She might be right; she is a chick after all. Don't they all think alike?

I rush out of the restaurant but there's no sign of Lucy. I run back to her apartment but it's still in darkness. I sit down on the front step and wait for her to come back.

I've fucked it up. I know I have.

Lucy

I'm slouched on the sofa, sobbing silent tears. I'm afraid to move because he'll hear me. I know he's out there. I'm guessing he's going to sit there all night, stubborn man that he is. I can't speak to him right now. As much as I wanted this to work I know I'm kidding myself. He's a bloody caveman. I can't do with the possessiveness or the jealousy, or even being told what I can and can't wear. It's not in my nature. I can't be that girl.

I won't be that girl.

Chapter Fourteen

Cowboy

After sitting on Lucy's doorstep for most of the night, I finally gave up and came back to the clubhouse at 2am. I'm pretty sure Lucy was in the apartment all along. I hope she was, I don't want to think where else she may have gone. I need to talk to her, but it's going to have to wait. Angel needs me to go on some club business with him, or I'd be back at Lucy's waiting to see her and tell her how sorry I am.

I'm pleased when I hear that Angel wants me to go with him to the bar in town and talk to the new owner. I know Lucy will be working. Hopefully I can kill two birds with one stone. I really don't want her working there, we don't know this Declan character. With all the shit that's going down around here I worry that I can't keep Lucy safe if she works there. It's something else we can't seem to agree on. Just one more thing on what's becoming a very long list.

We haven't been able to find out much at all about Declan. It's just too much of a coincidence he arrives on the scene at pretty much the same time as the drugs do. Prez doesn't want us going in mob handed though, he wants us to handle this diplomatically first just in case it is a coincidence.

The bar is busy with the Sunday lunch crowd and Lucy ignores me as she serves customers. I know she's seen me. When I try and catch her attention she just glares at me.

"Ouch." Angel snickers from behind me. I'd have come out with some smart retort if Declan hadn't noticed us enter. He walks over to greet us.

"Gentlemen, how can I help you? Table for two?" He smirks. He's a cocky little shit that's for sure. I look him up and down. Little probably isn't the right word to describe him. He's as tall as I am and as lean. He's all muscle. This guy knows how to take care of himself. Despite his young appearance there's something in his eyes that betrays his wisdom. As friendly as his smile is, he's cautious in his approach. Most people wouldn't notice it, but I have. He's constantly alert to his surroundings which tells me he hasn't been a bar owner for all of his professional life.

"Do you have a moment?" Angel enquires. "We'd like a little chat if you can spare the time." Damn my VP can sugar coat shit when he wants. I'd have gone n all guns blazing. Then I look at Lucy and realize that's where I'm going wrong. I need to act more like Angel, rather than a bull in a china shop. Angel knows how to treat a woman, not because he's had that many, but because he and Eve are solid. Everyone can see that. I could learn from my VP, but I'm no good at this soft shit. I'm not sure I could be, but looking at Lucy I tell myself I have to try.

Declan catches my gaze as I watch Lucy. She looks good today. "She's a good worker." He states. "I'd hate to see her get hurt." He looks me in the eye as he speaks. Angel senses my anger and places a restraining hand on my arm. What the fuck is it with everyone holding me back this weekend.

"I'd never hurt her." I growl.

"She's family." Angel states calmly. His eyes bore into Declan, a little of the politeness gone. "We take care of ours." His words are quiet, but the meaning behind them is loud and clear. It's an unspoken warning.

Declan just nods and turns to guide us to his office at the back of the bar. It's sparsely furnished, but what is in here looks like quality workmanship, like the rest of the bar. He's spared no expense, which tells me that he has money. I can't help wondering where it's come from.

"So how can I help you gentlemen?" He sits on the edge of his desk and gestures to two chairs in front of it for Angel and I to sit down.

"We've always kept a close eye on Severed and the people here. They come to us if they're in trouble and we take pride in keeping the town safe. Lately we've become concerned that there's a bad element coming in from somewhere." Angel offers, looking Declan in the eye as he speaks.

"And you think I'm that bad element?" Declan smirks in reply.

"I didn't say that." Angel says calmly.

"So what are you saying?" Declan crosses his arms and makes himself more comfortable against the desk.

"Why are you here?" I ask. Angel gives me a dirty look as my voice is clearly laced with disdain.

"A friend wanted to sell and I wanted a change of scenery." Declan isn't overly forthcoming with his reply.

"A change of scene from where?" Angel enquires.

"I think that's my business don't you?" Declan smirks again.

"We don't allow drugs in Severed." Angel states calmly, obviously bored with Declan's none answers. Declan's smirk falters for only a moment, but it's long enough for us both to notice. It's quickly replaced by a look of anger.

"I don't allow drugs in my bar." He grates out. I've never seen someone change so quickly. His whole face has darkened.

Angel takes the lead in the conversation. Declan remains pretty tight lipped about his past, but from what little he will tell us, it's clear he's lost someone close, to drugs. I'm not sure if that isn't why he wanted a change of scene.

As Angel fills him in on what's been happening in Severed I can see a change come over Declan. It's like a quiet anger takes over him.

"I caught someone dealing in here Friday night. I can assure you he won't be back any time soon." It's clear from his tone that the guy didn't just receive a verbal warning.

"I see." Angel nods. "I take it you hate drugs as much as we do."

"Despise them and the people who supply them." Declan growls back.

"So it's safe to say you're not the dealer?" I ask him.

"Look, I've never and will never have anything to do with that shit. It's up to you whether you believe me or not." He states calmly.

Angel and I exchange a look. We both believe him.

It's clear from the conversation that Declan is pretty switched on. He alludes to having contacts he can bring in to help get this problem sorted, but is evasive as to who or what they are. What is clear is that he's not behind this sudden drug incursion.

Before the conversation has ended I've found a grudging respect for the guy. He'll never be a best buddy, but he's an okay guy. I'm reassured that Lucy will be safe working here at least.

"I'll make sure Lucy gets home safely after her shift." He tells me as we're standing to leave. "From the look she gave you when you walked in I'm guessing you're not in her good books at the moment."

"Thanks." I mutter. Angel gives me one of his looks. The look that tells me I haven't heard the end of this and I'll have to explain myself when we get out of here. Shit.

I turn to head towards the bar but Declan stops me. "Let me have a word with her. Give her some space this afternoon." He suggests.

I know he means well but that doesn't stop me from wanting to smash my fist into his face, but he's right. I need to give her some space right now. Grudgingly I nod my agreement.

As we make our way out Lucy turns her back on me, but makes a point of waving goodbye to Angel.

When we reach the car park where our bikes are Angel stops me, "Okay, out with it Cowboy. What the fuck have you done to Lucy?"

As I look at my VP and try to figure out how to word it so I don't come out sounding like a total shit I realize I can't. I'm so fucking screwed.

Chapter Fifteen

Cowboy

The church room is full to capacity today. Prez has invited Carnal to the table to see if we can sort out the drug problem.

Scalp, Carnal's president, is here along with his VP Razor and a handful of close, trusted members. Just a year ago we'd never have been able to have this meeting, let alone in our clubhouse. There was too much friction between the clubs, all thanks to Satan. When I look over at Angel I can't believe that those two were related, never mind twins. They couldn't have been more different.

Scalp has been ribbing Prez about Teresa's pregnancy and the sleepless nights he's got ahead of him. It's good to see these guys getting on so well. I've got a lot of respect for Scalp, he suffered hell while Satan was alive like the rest of us, but he's managed to pull back the reins of his club.

Angel and Ink are the last ones to arrive and once they're seated Prez starts the meeting. He introduces Scalp and his guys, more as a formality than from necessity. We all know each other.

"So, VP. What news from the Strip Club?" Prez turns to look at Angel.

"You mean other than the fact Eve won't sleep with me since I went." He complains and looks at Ink who shrugs his shoulders as well.

"Same here Elle won't go near me since we went there. You've got to tell them we went under protest Prez." Ink pleads. The whole room breaks out in laughter at the sight of their faces. They look so hard done by.

"I'm serious Prez," Angel moans. "My old lady is fucking pissed."

"Never mind your fucking love lives or lack of," Prez laughs, "What's the news?"

The table goes serious again as Angel speaks.

"Cowboy and I have spoken to Declan at the pub. Although he won't tell us where he's from, I'm convinced he's clean. He's offered to bring in some manpower and help us get this sorted. I think he lost someone pretty close to him through drugs." Angel looks to me for approval and I nod.

"Yeah, I got that impression as well. He seemed pretty genuine to me." I offer. Doubt creeps in though, who am I to judge anyone, hell I couldn't even tell my best friend was behaving out of character and it got him killed.

"Ink and I spoke to Rick, the manager at the club. It's definitely new faces that are doing the dealing. He knew who Declan was, but said he didn't think it had anything to do with him and he certainly hadn't been around the joint." Angel pauses. "The girls weren't much help. They didn't want to admit they were buying as it could cost them their jobs if Rick finds out, but what we could get out of them is it's new blood. They're not good quality drugs either from the sound of it, that's why Tanya's dead. It was a bad fix as opposed to an overdose."

There are a few sad faces around the table. Tanya was always one of the more popular of the strippers.

"Bloody waste." Someone mutters and there are murmurs of agreement.

"You heard anything Scalp?" Prez asks him. All heads turn to hear his reply.

"Same as your guys really. Whoever it is it's new blood and it's poor quality. From what we can see they're storing the drugs somewhere locally and its hoods they've brought in with them that are doing the dealing. No one's heard who's heading this up."

"Fuck." Prez curses. None of us want drugs here in Severed. Aside from anything else it will bring crime here, like the addict who robbed Sue to get enough money for his next fix.

"It's your turf." Scalp continues. "We'll do whatever you need to get this sorted. Touch wood its not reached Carnal yet and I for one want to keep it that way."

It's one thing Carnal offering their support, but right now we're fighting a hidden enemy. Declan seemed confident his sources could come up with some Intel for us, but I'm still not sure I trust him. I don't know him well enough,

Prez calls the meeting to order and we all start to drift slowly out to the bar. Angel and Ink collar him in the back of the room though, preventing him from leaving.

"Come on boss, don't be a cockblocker." I hear Ink complain. I let out a loud laugh. Angel and Ink really have had some shit from their women over the Str p Club business.

"Fine, fine. If you guys can't handle your fucking women folk then I guess I'll have to take care of it for you." Prez laughs loudly as he swaggers out of the room.

Angel and Ink exchange a victorious glance. I don't know why those two are looking so happy. I know Eve and Elle and if they think Prez telling their old ladies that he ordered the guys to go to the Strip Club is going to fix it, they've got a long wait coming.

Those guys are about to get handed their balls on a plate by the girls. Then again, maybe they already have.

Chapter Sixteen

Angel

I'm suffering blue balls, even though Prez kept his promise and spoke to the girls. Apparently that's not enough and Eve still won't let me near her. I don't think she'll be fucking happy until she's had me disinfected after visiting that place. Fucking women.

I'm hiding out at the tattoo shop, as I can't bear being in the house with Eve and not being allowed to touch her. It's lucky for her that Sue is still staying with us or I'd have shown her who was boss and dragged her to bed. There's only so much I can take and this is fucking killing me.

As I'm torturing myself thinking about Eve, something outside catches my attention. Keeping my eyes on the street I try to get Ink's attention.

"Ink" I hiss. "Come here." Looking out of the window I can't believe what I'm seeing. Some cocky little shit is dealing drugs in front of the café over the street. I can't believe the fucking nerve of him. It's bad enough he's dealing this shit out in the open but to do it in front of the tattoo shop is downright suicidal.

Ink saunters over to see what I wanted him for. "Fucking idiot has some balls." He exclaims.

I motion over one of the prospects who's sitting leafing through one of the design magazines.

"See that fucker over there?" He nods his head in acknowledgement. "I'm going to go over there and have a word with him. I want you to stay out of sight and when I'm done I want you to follow him. I want to know where he goes, who he sees and even when he stops to take a piss. You got me?"

The prospect nods in understanding. I motion for Ink to join me and we step out of the shop and cross the road. Now I'm not being vain but Ink and I are a pretty imposing sight, but this little shit doesn't even flinch when we stop in front of him. He just graces us with a nod of his head.

"Gentlemen." He nods at us. "What can I do you for?" I could laugh in his fucking face, he thinks we're here to buy drugs!

I grab him by his shirt collar and physically lift him from the ground so we're at eye level. "You can get the fuck out of my town and take that shit with you." I thunder.

He doesn't even flinch. When I drop him back to his feet he simply shrugs his shoulders and straightens the collar on his shirt.

"I don't think you gentlemen know who you're messing with." He smirks. "There's a new boss in town and you'd do well to accept that." I want to wipe the smirk from the little shits face.

"And I don't think you know who you're dealing with." Ink stands tall. "This is our town and we don't do drugs. Take that back to your boss and get the fuck out of here." He snarls.

"Gentlemen." The dealer simply nods his head at us as though he were some southern gentleman wishing us a good day. As much as I want to give this little shit a beating I hold back. He's more use to us if we let him go and find out who's behind this.

I see the prospect exit the shop and follow at a discreet distance as the dealer walks away.

"That guy had no fear." Ink looks shocked. I guess I am too. On his own Ink is pretty intimidating but the two of us together should have put the fear of god in the guy. It leaves me with a sickening feeling. Who the fuck are we dealing with that his lackeys aren't even scared of us?

Chapter Seventeen

Lucy

I'm not really sure why Eve called me down to the clubhouse this afternoon. She came out with some bullshit excuse about Teresa being bored and needing company, but I get the impression there's some ulterior motive behind the call. I agreed to meet them anyway.

It's pretty quiet out in the yard. We're enjoying the late afternoon sun and aside from the prospects on the gates it's just us girls out here.

Elle starts to laugh about the way Prez had pulled her and Eve aside to let them know that he was the one who insisted Ink and Angel went to the Strip Club.

"Of course I knew it was him, but it's far too much fun watching Ink stew." She laughs. "Don't you dare give in just yet." She instructs Eve.

"Don't worry. I'm not." Eve joins in the laughter. "It won't do my bruising any harm not to be bouncing around in bed for a while." I splutter into my drink at Eve's openness.

I love these women; they speak so freely about their men and their love lives. I guess it's because they're confident in the love their men have for them. They all have a kind of glow about them and I don't mean Teresa's pregnancy glow, there's just something about them that radiates happy and contented.

"Wel I'm glad Prez didn't go." Teresa offers. "There's no way in hell I'm cutting him off while I'm this fucking horny." We all break out in laughter at that. "I'm serious guys. I think this baby is going to be a boy. I mean it has to be if it's making me this horny!" She turns to Eve. "Were you this bad"

As soon as the question is asked we all go quiet. I wasn't here to witness it, but I know the pain that Eve went through. No woman should have to go through that.

"Ah shit. I'm sorry honey." Teresa's face is full of guilt as she strokes Eve's hair.

Eve shakes her head. "No, it's okay. Really." She takes a deep breath. "Both times no. I mean Elizabeth's dad was a dick anyway so I just wasn't interested and well, the second time I didn't even know, but as far as I remember it wasn't any different."

Eve shrugs her shoulders and smiles. Elle starts to choke on her food and then we're all laughing.

"It's a good job my gag reflex isn't this bad when I'm giving a blow job." Elle winks. Just like that the awkward moment has passed.

I do enjoy the company of these women, they're good medicine for my troubled soul.

Teresa complains about how fat she's getting but is quickly hushed by Eve and Elle who tell her how beautiful she looks and what a great job she's doing growing this baby.

"I'm not a fucking oven or a propagator." She whines. "I mean I can't even see my feet now." I know Teresa's scared of becoming a mother. Personally I think she's too selfish to be a parent just now, although I hope that will change when she has the baby. It's only a couple of months away now.

"Well I envy you." Elle declares, placing a hand on Teresa's protruding belly. "I think it must be amazing to be pregnant, to be giving life to a new human being." She sounds almost wistful. I kind of get where she's coming from, but it's not something I'd be rushing into wanting any time soon.

"Pffft." Teresa snorts. "You have the fucking baby then." She huffs herself to her feet. "I need to pee again." She complains, then her face lights up. "I might just see if my hubby is around to service me after." She grins.

Eve and Elle are shaking their heads at her as she waddles off into the clubhouse. As soon as the door is shut behind her they turn their attention on me.

"Soooo Lucy." Elle draws out the so. "What's with you and Cowboy then?"

I groan. "There's nothing going on." I protest. From the look on their faces I'm not getting away with it. "We thought there could be, but he's such an arrogant, jealous ..." I can't think of more words to portray how I feel. "God, he gets me so angry."

"It's luurve." Eve chimes.

"No it's not." I snap.

"Oh trust me girl. It's love." Elle joins in, wiggling her eyebrows. "You two are meant to be, anyone can see it."

I flush at the thought of these people watching me and Cowboy interact, of them thinking something is there that isn't.

"We tried. It was a total fuck up." I tell them. I go on to let them know about his constant instruction on my life, his demands over my job, my clothing and then end with the fiasco at the restaurant.

"Give him a second chance." Eve pleads. "Trust me, he's a good guy."

"He's a bloody great guy." Elle adds.

"I know he s." I offer sadly. "We just rub each other up the wrong way."

"Maybe you need to get naked and rub each other the right way." Elle laughs and Eve joins in.

The laughter dies away when they see I'm not joining in.

"He's had a really hard time of it this year." Eve sounds sad. "He's lost some people really close to him and he just needs time and someone to help him heal from that." She turns to look at me, all serious now. "I think you're that person Lucy."

I get where the girls are coming from and tell them that. But I'm still convinced that I'm not the kind of girl that Cowboy needs. I don't even embrace the whole biker lifestyle like these two do.

I look around at the yard full of bikes and scrunch my face in frustration. "Does the biker lifestyle bother you?" Eve asks intuitively.

"Am I that obvious?" I ask.

"Honey, neither of us even knew bikers before we met these guys." Elle tells me. "They have a habit of growing on you and I have to say I love the family that comes with it." She smiles contentedly. From the little I know Elle never really had a family of her own growing up. "You just need to know how to control them." She laughs.

"We all know how well I get along with bikes." Eve offers while rubbing her bruise.

"But you guys control them in the bedroom." I blurt out. Shit. I can't believe I just said that to them.

"Exactly." Eve laughs. "We let them think they're in control, all alpha male and shit, but when it counts we've got them wrapped round our little fingers."

I think back to the conversation earlier, how the girls are withholding sex because of the Strip Club trip and I realize that they do hold some control after all.

"I guess I was afraid that I'd have to give up being me." I offer sadly. "I've only just found me, or the person I want to be. I don't want to give it up so quickly."

For years I've acted the way I thought I should. How my parents expected me to behave, being influenced by friends. It went further when I started to date and that's when I realized you shouldn't change for a man. I'm not ready to give up my freedom and control over my life just yet.

"You don't have to stop being you." Eve tells me. "It's you that Cowboy's fallen for and trust me that guy's fallen for you alright." She pulls me into a hug. "We all love you just as you are, don't change that. Just give him a little time to adjust to the idea is all." She suggests.

Elle points at the clubhouse. "You see this? We didn't sign up for this, we didn't have a clue what we were letting ourselves in for when we met these guys, but now... now we wouldn't be without them, or without the club. We belong." She joins in the group hug, its too much for the bench we're on and we all fall onto the ground just as Teresa comes out of the door sulking.

"Bloody man has business to attend to." She complains.

We all burst out laughing at her, I don't think any of us understands why, we're just in a silly mood after the conversation we just had I guess.

Teresa shuffles her way back to the table and looks down on us lying in the dust.

"Okay bitches, if this is a group hug you'll have to bring it up here to me. I can't get my fat ass down there anymore." She smiles.

We stand and wrap arms around each other. The girls are right. This place does feel like home.

Chapter Eighteen

Cowboy

Angel and I are watching Ink set out his needles and shit when we're interrupted. There's an almighty smash from the front of the shop and we all rush into the reception area together. I guess I'm lucky Ink hadn't started work on my new tattoo yet, although he'd got the gun in his hand ready. I will get this bloody tat one day if it kills me.

The window at the front of the store is smashed inwards. There's glass all over the floor.

"What the hell!" Ink roars. "I've only just had that fucking window replaced." Suddenly we're all brought back to the day when Rachel died here in the shop.

CARNAL PERSUASION (SEVERED MC #4)

"I thought you replaced it with toughened glass?" I ask

"Fucking supplier can't get his head out of his ass and get it here." Ink grumbles.

He stoops to pick something up from the floor. It's a large rock. Someone's done this deliberately.

"Fuck!" Angel roars looking through the remains of the window. *What now?* I follow his gaze and am suddenly furious.

Some fucking shit has slashed the tires on all of our bikes outside. Someone is definitely going to pay for this.

"Who?" Ink looks to us both for an answer.

"I'm guessing this is to do with the fucking drug gang or whatever the hell they are." Angel groans. No one else would be stupid enough to do this on our doorstep after all.

Ink's on the phone, I think he's shouting at the prospect that was following the drug dealer they hassled earlier. He doesn't look happy.

"Find him, now." He commands quietly, before hanging up the call.

"It was that fucking drug dealer from earlier. Stupid prospect watched him do it!" Ink's getting so irate his face is going red. "And then he fucking lost him!"

"I'll deal with him later." Angel advises him. "Let's get this mess cleared up, get the bikes fixed and go get a drink." He suggests.

Ink brings the boards from the back storeroom and Angel and I get to work putting them up over the front window. One of the prospects sweeps the broken glass from the floor, while Ink is on the phone giving the glass supplier hell and telling him he's not paying for the repair this time. If they'd installed the toughened glass when he ordered it then this wouldn't have happened.

Cherry soon arrives with the truck to take the bikes back to the compound. Ink, Angel and I head over to the bar. We're all in need of a drink right now and we can see if Declan's managed to find anything out since our last visit.

Chapter Nineteen

Cowboy

"So you had your window smashed and the tyres on all your bikes slashed?" Declan asks.

"Yep." Angel leans back in the booth Declan ushered us into when we arrived.

I think he could tell we were all pretty pissed off. I can't believe the fuckers messed with our bikes!

I take a big gulp of my beer hoping it will calm me, but it doesn't work. This is so fucked up. Why can't we break free of this run of bad luck? I'm not sure I can take much more of this year.

"You boys sure lead interesting lives." Declan laughs.

"Unfortunately." Ink grumbles. Declan looks a little confused.

"We just want a simple life Dec, but we can never seem to catch a break lately." Angel speaks for us all.

"Oh right," Declan nods. "But you're motorcycle enthusiasts who don't mind getting their hands dirty?"

Angel looks serious. "When we're pushed, we'll do anything to protect our family."

We've spent several hours drinking beer and wondering why shit's happening, when the pub doors burst open. I look up to see one of the prospects running in our direction.

"VP." He sounds relieved. "I went by the tattoo shop, but you weren't there."

Ange frowns. "Phone?"

The prospect fidgets. "The batteries dead."

Angel leans his head back in frustration.

"Fucking hell prospect." I growl at him. Dude fucking never remembers to charge his phone.

"I know, I'm sorry." He looks shit scared so I leave him alone.

"What did you need me so desperately for?" Angel asks.

"I lost that dealer. He literally vanished. I can't fucking find him anywhere." He looks nervous at sharing this with us .The poor guy looks like shit. He tells us he's been trying to find him for the past few hours since he broke the window and trashed the bikes. When Angel looks at me and rolls his eyes, I know he's thinking the same as me. The kid deserves a break. See, we're not always so bad.

Angel's phone begins to ring as Declan hands the prospect a beer.

"Prez." He answers. I watch him as he listens to Prez, he doesn't look happy. "On our way."

He hangs up the phone and gulps down the rest of his beer, so I follow his lead. It looks like we need to go.

"We gotta run, Declan. Thanks for the beers." Angel stands and we all follow.

"No problem" Declan shakes our VP's hand. "I'll get onto my contacts again. I'm sorry I didn't have any news for you today. We need to get to the bottom of this."

Ange expresses his gratitude. As we walk out the bar I think that this guy really isn't as bad as I first thought.

CARNAL PERSUASION (SEVERED MC #4)

Once we get outside, Angel stands to face us. "Prez wants us back at the clubhouse right now. Seems we have some unwanted visitors."

"Who?" I ask.

"The police." Angel replies as he jumps into the truck.

"What the fuck? Why?" Ink asks.

"He didn't say." Angel answers. "I guess it's to do with what happened at the shop earlier."

The drive back is quiet and tense. It's not a long drive, so we're soon pulling up in front of the clubhouse.   It's not one of the police guys we know.

"Fuck." Angel quietly grinds out before exiting ahead of us and charging across the yard. He quickly makes his way over to Prez. We all follow as swiftly as we can, but fuck the VP is fast! "What's going on here?" He asks.

Prez gestures at the arrogant looking police man standing beside him. He stinks of dickhead, so I know this isn't going to go well.

"This here is officer Dirk." Prez introduces him. I hear chuckling from behind me.

"Dirk?" Ice snickers quietly and Kid laughs along.

I fight to hide my own smile as the guys behind me are cracking some hilarious jokes and it hasn't gone unnoticed.

"Mature friends you have." Officer Dirk says to Prez.

Prez just smiles back.

"Why are you here?" Angel asks earning him a glare from the officer.

"I'm here to question you all about Steven Brook." He looks really fucking smug.

We all look at each other in confusion, we thought he was here about the damage at the tattoo shop, but don't say anything. Prez asks, "Who?"

The officer stands taller as he stares us down. "Do you know Steven Brook?" We all shake our heads. "Any of you?"

"Look, we don't know who you're talking about." Prez informs him.

"You got a picture?" Angel asks. Officer Dirk motions to the pretty little police officer behind him, she reaches into a folder and passes him some small pieces of paper.

He turns one over and shows it to Angel and Prez. Prez doesn't react at all, but Angel does. It's subtle. He's lucky Officer Dirk was looking at Prez and not him. I saw his eyes widen and his jaw tighten. He quickly controls himself and shows no emotion.

Officer Dirk isn't happy with his lack of results and shows the rest of us the picture. I see why Angel reacted like he did. The photo shows a bloodied body. There are cuts and slashes everywhere, but under the blood I'm able to recognize him as the drug dealer we saw outside the tattoo shop.

"Where were you today between two and four?" He asks us all.

"I was here and there's plenty of people to confirm that.' Prez coolly replies.

"We were at the bar down town." Angel answers. Officer Dirk smirks.

"Anyone to confirm that?" God I'd love to punch the arrogant prick to the floor.

"Yep." Angel answers just as smugly. "Declan, the bar manager."

The officer stills. "The new owner?"

"The very same." Angel answers.

Officer Dirk hands the pictures back to his co-worker then nods at us. "Ok gentlemen, I'll follow that up. I'll be back if I need to ask you any more questions."

As soon as they drive off Prez looks to us. "We have a problem here?"

Angel shakes his head. "No, but we do know him."

"How?"

"The dead guy in the pictures is the drug dealer we saw dealing and the same guy who trashed the window and bikes at the tattoo shop."

"Fuck!" Prez shouts. "You do this?" He asks. Angel looks pissed.

"Fuck no!" He yells.

"Only asking, VP." Prez looks up to the sky. "We need to find out who did."

"Shouldn't we have been given a heads up before the police turned up?" Ice asks. He's right. We have a couple of police officers that are sympathetic to the way we take care of Severed and they normally keep us in the loop.

"Yeah we should." Prez pulls out his phone. "I think it's time to call Carnal and have another get together because this shit is getting worse." He mutters as he storms off.

Chapter Twenty

Cowboy

Walking into the clubhouse bar, we hear Prez shout from his office.

"VP!"

Angel leaves while we get our drinks. The ice-cold beer goes down well and I smack my lips in appreciation. Ink looks at me like I'm mad and I just smile back.

"So who do you think is behind the murder?" he asks me.

"No fucking clue." I reply.

"You know," Cherry interrupts. "I wouldn't be surprised if it was his boss. For fucking up."

I think it over and nod my head. "Good point."

"I can't believe that guy is dead." Ink says. "Not saying it's a bad thing."

"Fuck, did you see that picture? Made me feel a little sick." Cherry rubs his stomach.

"Pussy." Ink laughs.

"Shut up about it." I snap. Fucking children.

It's a good job they change the subject as Prez and Angel come back just then. Neither of them looks very happy.

Prez stands in front of us. From the way he's standing he means business.

"Get ready because we're going out. Are your bikes fixed?" He smiles, but it's not a pleased smile.

"Where?" Ink asks.

"Carnal." Angel answers. There's a moments silence until I break it.

"Well shit."

Prez nods at me. "Yeah. You three need to get ready because we're leaving now. We need to get to the bottom of this shit."

Less than ten minutes later, we're on our way to the Carnal clubhouse. I'd be lying if I said this wasn't strange. I've never visited Carnal for anything good and I've never been in the clubhouse before.

When we pull up in front of their gates they're opened straight away for us by a couple of members who actually smile when they see us. Told you, fucking weird.

Carnal's clubhouse is slightly smaller than ours and it's painted black. It looks dark and unwelcoming. Scalp greets us at the front door and ushers us inside. Leaving Cherry outside to guard the bikes, Prez, Angel, Ink and me follow him through to the back of the club.

I don't know how Carnal members cope because it's so dark in here. There are some club whores lounging around. I much prefer our girls. These look slightly gothic and a little on the rough side.

"Fuck," Ink whispers behind me. "These chicks look like dominatrix."

I can't help but laugh, although I can see where he's coming from.

Scalp leads us into the large church room where some of the Carnal members are waiting for us. They're all sitting at one end of the table, leaving the other empty for us. Scalp sits at his end, with Prez sitting at the other both of them flanked by their VP's and Sergeant at Arms.

We all nod a greeting to each other and then Scalp calls the meeting to order.

"Welcome Severed. While you're here, please treat this place like your home." He grins.

"Prez and I called this meeting because there have been some new developments at the Severed end." Scalp advises.

Everyone looks to Prez. "I asked for this meeting because we had the police at our clubhouse this afternoon. Seems there's been a murder and they have Angel and Cowboy here as suspects."

Nobody says anything and Prez raises his eyebrows. "You hear anything around here Scalp? One of the drug dealers was murdered? It was the one we saw dealing who trashed the tattoo shop and some of our bikes earlier today?"

Scalp nods his head. "Yeah, I know who you're talking about."

"What can you tell us?" Angel asks.

Scalp takes a deep breath. "I already knew he'd been murdered because my VP is responsible."

"What the fuck?" Angel shouts. "You couldn't give us a heads up?"

Razor, Carnal's VP steps in. "We haven't had time. I've been trying to tie up some loose ends."

"What loose ends?" Prez asks.

"We caught him dealing a bit too close to home. We were just having a friendly chat, but he didn't quite see it that way." Razor shrugs his shoulders.

"You threatened him." Scalp interrupts.

"And were your loose ends witnesses?" Angel guesses.

"Yeah. The kid he was selling to. When he'd finished dealing I followed him. When he was alone I tried to get some intel out of him but he was a tough nut and wasn't talking. I couldn't let him walk away after that."

"Fucking hell." Prez grumbles.

"Anything else to add?" I ask.

"I've haven't been able to find the kid he was selling to yet. He might have recognized us." Razor admits.

"How the fuck do you all survive?" Angel asks. "How fucking stupid are you?"

Razor glares at Angel. "You ain't all that perfect Angel so back the fuck off!"

"Alright, lets cool it." Prez warns. "At least we know who it was now."

There's nothing much left to share at the table. Neither club knows who's behind the drugs and now we've lost our only lead with the dead dealer.

Despite the animosity between Angel and Razor we're all still on pretty good terms, so we accept Scalp's invitation to stay and have a drink with them.

As we stand to leave the table there's good-natured banter between us. Scalp calls Prez over to his side of the room so they can confer privately, club leader to club leader and the rest of us move towards the door to cement our new partnership over a cold beer.

Chapter Twenty One

Cherry

I'm bored as shit sitting here watching the bikes while the rest of the guys have their little powwow in the clubhouse. There's a nice distraction when one of the Carnal club whores comes over and starts paying some attention to me.

She's wearing denim shorts that aren't fastened. They're so short they reveal most of her ample ass cheeks. The soft fraying of the hems that decorate her cream skin are inviting me to touch. I almost do, but then remember my old lady Sam. She'd have my dick on a plate if she found out. I still watch her though as she bites down on her lip and moves closer to me. I find myself imagining where that open V of material is leading to. She makes a point of tracing her finger from her

CARNAL PERSUASION (SEVERED MC #4)

exposed waist up to her breasts. Her top is a cropped shirt that's overly tight on her chest, not that I'm complaining. I suspect her cleavage is artificially created by the too small bra she's wearing underneath.

"Hi." She greets me. I snap my eyes from her breasts. She seems pretty pleased at my attention as a wide smile appears on her face. "I'm Kirsty."

She's got long dark hair and brown eyes like my Sam, but that's where the similarity ends. Kirsty isn't ugly, but Sam's better looking. Kirsty looks a lot older on closer inspection, she's been around the block a few times I reckon. I bet she knows how to treat a biker. I'm guessing she's had a lot of practice.

"Cherry." I greet her.

"Cherry?" She laughs, twirling her hair around her finger. "I like it."

"I'm pleased to hear that darlin'." I smile at her.

"So you're from Severed?" I nod in answer. "You're a good looking bunch of bikers aren't you."

She eyes me greedily and trails her finger down my chest. What can I say? I'm a man. A man who can't say no when it's offered up to me. Kirsty flatters me and makes me feel wanted. The opposite of how things are at home right now. Sam seems a little touchy these days and definitely less affectionate. That's why, when Kirsty reaches for my zip and sinks to her knees, I don't stop her. We're on Carnal turf and Sam will never find out. What's to lose?

Kirsty reaches greedily for my cock, working me hard and when she's happy she then wraps her red glossed lips around it. I hear her moan with satisfaction as she takes me in her mouth. Her gag reflex is pretty poor for a whore and she can't take me fully. She does a passable enough blowjob, good enough to make me come. I smirk when she swallows my come down her throat and chokes a little. She's nothing like my Sam. I come to my senses at the thought of Sam. My body freezes at the thought of my old lady. *Shit*. She's going to kill me when she finds out. I push Kirsty away, but she doesn't seem to notice the slight.

I'm just fastening my cock back into my jeans when I hear a noise. Before I have time to work out where it came from a figure comes rushing past in a blur. They pound into Kirsty who squeals as she falls, knocking us both to the ground. I try to stand up, but Kirsty has landed awkwardly on top of me. Pushing her off I finally get to my feet and look around to find whoever just sent me flying.

I see a guy with a black ski mask over his head. I reach for my gun, but it's too fucking late. Whatever he had in his hands is gone. He threw one into the workshop and one through a window of the clubhouse. Fuck. This can't be good.

I let off a shot but it misses. It does draw the attention of a couple of Carnal members though who have just drifted out into the yard. The meeting must be over. They take chase, but the guy's gone. He vaulted over the fence and straight into a waiting car that screeches off.

I'm thrown back to the floor again as there's a loud crashing bang from the clubhouse and black smoke starts to fill the yard. Less than a second later the workshop blows. I cover my face to hide from the flying debris. Judging by the flames and flying burning debris there were welding gas tanks in there.

There's a ringing in my ears and my sight is a little blurry as I manage to slowly get back up.

As the smoke starts to settle I can see that the back wall of the clubhouse has gone, collapsed inwards. The Carnal guys that were outside are trying to douse the flames in the workshop. The noise is deafening. There are bits of burning ash everywhere in the air.

I'm in shock looking at the carnage around me. Kirsty is still on the floor, staring open mouthed at the flames bursting from what little remains of the workshop.

Suddenly instinct kicks in. My Prez and brothers are in that clubhouse, or what's left of it. Please God, let them be alright I pray as I turn and run hell for leather to find them.

Chapter Twenty Two

Cowboy

I'm almost out of the room when there's a crash from the window. Turning I can see that Prez and Scalp are standing just in front of it and looking in shock at something on the floor.

"Shit!" Scalp shouts and starts to dive to the side.

"Get down!" Prez shouts.

I look at the floor and see what looks like a dark green metallic tennis ball with writing on the side. What the fuck?

Suddenly there's a loud popping noise and the room fills with burning spots of light. I'm thrown backwards through the door. As I hit the floor with a thud there's an even louder sound from outside and I feel the ground shake beneath me. It sounds like all hell has broken loose out there.

Stunned, I lay there for a moment, trying to work out what the fuck just happened. My hearing is clouded and it's hard to see as the room is full of acrid black smoke. Through what's left of the outside wall I can see a building on fire. Planks of burning wood are flying towards us.

Everything's happening in slow motion, yet it can only have been seconds since I saw the green metal object on the floor. As my hearing starts to return I can hear women's terrified screaming and sobbing, as well as groans and cussing from the bikers around me.

I look around me to see who's hurt. I can see Angel and Ink moving towards me. They see me at the same time I see them. There's blood pouring from a cut on Angel's head and Ink is covered in cuts and grazes but they look okay apart from that.

Angel reaches me first and holds out a hand to help me to my feet.

"You okay?" He looks me up and down, surveying for damage I guess. I do my own cursory check. I ache like a motherfucker, but nothing appears to be broken.

"Yeah, I think so." I glance at Ink. "You guys?"

"Yeah, we'll live." Ink mutters. "What the fuck was that?" He looks around the clubhouse, or what's left standing of it.

The whole back wall of the clubhouse is gone. What I think was the workshop is a ball of flame. The back wall is where the church room was located.

"Fuck! Prez!" I yell. Angel and Ink look at me, understand dawning. I start to panic. Prez was standing in front of that wall when it all went to shit. There's nothing there now but a pile of rubble. There's no sign of Scalp either. Shit.

Frantically we rush to where I think I last saw Prez. It's a pile of bricks, dust and smoke. Broken remnants of the once solid table litter the area. The clubs flag hangs in tatters from one of the remaining walls. It's one of the saddest sights I've ever seen. We haven't got time to think of that right now though, we need to find Prez.

Razor and Viper are right behind us. We're shouting for Prez and they're calling for Scalp.

One by one we slowly remove the rubble from the area. It's slow going, as we don't know what we're going to find underneath. In the distance we can hear the faint sound of sirens coming closer.

There's not enough room for any one else in here, so the five of us work side by side. We pass the rubble back, the other club members forming a human chain to clear the debris from the area.

We work quickly, efficiently and in total silence. No one dare say what we're all thinking. There's too much rubble. There's no way anyone could have survived standing in front of that wall. If it had happened just five minutes earlier it would have been much worse, the room was full. That said, how can it be any worse than losing Prez?

My throat is raw from the smoke and dust, my fingers shredded from the broken bricks and glass we're removing. My eyes are stinging from the smoke and I ache like a bitch from the force of being thrown backwards, but I carry on. We've got to find them.

"Here!" Viper shouts from a little to our left. There's a scrap of denim showing. It could be either of them. We concentrate on the area, working as quickly as we can; yet still being safe.

"Fuck no!" There's a scream from my side. "Get some fucking help in here now. No!" His painful cries fill what's left of the room. "He can't be dead. No. No. No."

I turn and look down into the face of the man I once knew. *This can't be happening,* I think as his lifeless eyes stare back at me.

Chapter Twenty Three

Cowboy

As I get off my bike I look at the house in front of us. We're here to deliver terrible news to his old lady. I don't want to be here. This is going to be fucking hard. What we're about to tell her will destroy her family. I can hardly bear the weight of that pain.

I follow Angel, letting him take the lead. I can tell he's dreading this as much as I am. I can see him mentally preparing himself. He looks around and I know past memories of being here are haunting him. Some demons never leave you.

We hear the squeak of the door and look to see her standing there, waiting to greet us like the good old lady she is. She smiles at us both. God, it makes my heart hurts. She has no fucking idea the hell we re about to deliver to her. It's going to slam into her like a bulldozer. In a matter of seconds her life will be ripped apart.

She must see our grave expressions as we make our way over to her. Her welcoming smile fades away and in its place is fear. This is bringing back so many memories that I'd rather not think about. I've tried so hard to keep them buried so I can carry on with life, but I know it's not right. I'm going to have to face up to them all, but I'm just not ready for it. Not yet. Being here and knowing why, this shit is just making it all worse.

She looks scared, almost as if she knows why we're here. That's the lifestyle for you. Us men do the dirty work, but the women in our lives are the strong ones. Don't let our size and tattoos fool you because it's the women who hold us up. When fate steps in to end us, it's those women we've left behind that have to keep everything together. The old ladies who can handle this life have my respect.

I reach out and touch his arm. "Angel? You sure we should be the ones to do this?"

I'm thinking there are other people that should be the ones to tell her that her old man has died. I don't think I can. How can I? I can hardly handle my own grief these days, never mind helping someone else cope with theirs.

Angel turns to face me. I see the sadness in his eyes. He shakes his head. "I owe this to her. It should be me; I need to be here for her. She's my family." He takes a deep breath. "Besides, that's my nephew in there."

His words hit me hard as I watch him look over at the house. He sees James in the window waving at us. James jumps up and down, happy to see us as we both return his wave. His smile widens and my heart hurts more than I ever fucking thought possible.

James looks so much like his dad which means he also looks like Angel. Angel laughs at James greeting, but there's no heart to it. It's a sad kind of laugh. He knows the pain we're about to bring into that little boys life. He hasn't had a great start, poor guy. Being the son of the evilest man I have ever met and then having his birth mother turn into a revengeful evil bitch. Not that he ever knew them as his parents. Scalp's the only dad he's known. Scalp and Maggie took him on and cared for him as their own.

Gathering myself I follow Angel until he reaches Maggie. They greet each other with a hug and she gives me a sweet smile over Angel's shoulder. All I can manage is a small smile in return. I just can't. I'm not good with grief. Why the fuck did Angel bring me with him?

"Hi guys." Maggie greets. "You want to come in for a drink?"

"Erm," Angel begins. "Not right now."

Going inside would probably be the best way to deliver our sac news, rather than here, but James is inside and none of us would want him to hear this.

Maggie looks at both of us. "If you're here for Scalp then he's out already, but you're more than welcome to stay and wait. He shouldn't be long."

Oh fuck. She thinks we're here to see Scalp.

Shit, shit shit!

"Maggie, I know Scalp isn't here." He tries to explain, but stops. This is hard for him. "We were over at Carnal having a meeting with him when there was an explosion."

"Explosion?" She gasps. Angel nods his head. "Oh my god! Is everyone ok? Where's Scalp?" For the first time she seems to take in our disheveled appearance. We're both dirty and covered in dust and grime from earlier. We came straight here.

"That's why we're here babe. He was trapped under the rubble."

"Is he okay?" Maggie asks hesitantly. It's almost silent but I still hear her panicked plea to God for him to be okay.

"I'm sorry Maggie, we tried." Angel has a halting sob in his voice now. "By the time we found him and dug him out he wasn't breathing."

All I hear is a deep inhale of breath and then Angel has to react quickly as Maggie falls. He catches her n his arms, holding her up as tears start to fall down her face.

"No, it can't be. You've got it wrong." She demands. "If it was real then it would be Viper standing here, not you."

"I'm sorry." Angel whispers. "Viper wanted to come, but you and James are family Maggie. I told him it should be me that came to tell you. Viper's gone to the hospital with him. He'll make sure they take care of him and deal with all the formalities for you babe."

Maggie sags in his arms and really begins to sob as it starts to sink in.

I can see her pain and as her screams become louder, I can feel it. I have to look away. Seeing her hurting like this is too much for me to handle. In a flash the memories of friends that I have lost come back to me and just like Maggie, I almost fall to the floor from the impact.

I hear a quiet knocking and look up to see that I'm in front of the window James is looking through. He can't see his mum because of the angle, so he's still smiling broadly. He waves; looking really excited to see me. I smile and wave back at him.

The little guy needs to smile as much as he can right now because soon I don't think he'll have much reason to. He needs to be strong for his mum now.

Rest in peace Scalp, I'll miss you, you big scary looking bastard.

Chapter Twenty Four

Cowboy

There's something about funerals, they remind you of your own mortality, of opportunities you've missed or just let slide through your fingers. I look at Lucy standing beside me and realize that I can't let her be one of those lost opportunities.

"Is Teresa not coming?" She looks up at me.

I shake my head, sorrow in my heart. "No, it's too much for her."

Teresa is too close to her due date. The news about Prez has left her a mess. At this time in her pregnancy she should be the happiest she's ever been. Hearing about Scalp and more importantly Prez has ripped that happiness away from her.

Teresa has locked herself away inside their room at the clubhouse. She won't speak to any of the guys, just her girls. I think she blames us for what happened to Prez. I think that's why she doesn't want to see us. We've tried telling her that it wasn't our fault, but she just gets pissed at us and tells us to leave.

All this can't be good for her baby, she shouldn't have to be experiencing this.

As the graveside service comes to an end I look over at Maggie. She's just standing by the graveside, sobbing her heart out. I can't begin to imagine the pain she's going through. James is standing by Maggie's side, the odd tear sliding down his cheek as he holds his mothers hand with his tiny one. He's trying to be strong for his mother. It's sad because he's way too young to have to be living through this.

"It doesn't feel right James being here." Lucy whispers to me.

I nod in agreement. "Yes, but he seems to have the same stubborn streak as his uncle."

"I heard that." Angel snaps quietly from my other side.

Never mind James attending, I know Lucy didn't want to be here. She feels out of place, as though she doesn't belong. After everything that's happened I've decided Lucy's place is by my side, I just need to work out how to tell her that.

I managed to convince her that she's part of the Severed family and that we all need to be here to pay our respects to our fallen friend.

There's as many of the Severed members and their families here today as there are from Carnal. Scalp was a good guy when it came down to it, a good leader.   We'll all miss him.

"I feel like I should be back at the clubhouse with Teresa. I don't like the thought of her all alone right now." Lucy says softly.

I watch Elle takes Lucy's hand in hers. She and Ink are standing on the other side of Lucy. "She's fine. We took her to the hospital before we came here. She'll be okay now she's with Prez."

Prez was lucky; he managed to survive the explosion that killed Scalp. However it's not all good news. After we found Scalp we quickly uncovered Prez next. He was near death. If the ambulance hadn't already been there waiting when we found him, I dread to think what would have happened. He's not come round yet, he's in a deep coma and nobody knows how long for, or even if he'll make it. It's tearing Teresa and the rest of us apart. We can't lose Prez; it doesn't even bear thinking about.

After sitting by his bedside for a full twenty-four hours, Teresa finally broke down and had to leave. She couldn't bear to look at her old man lying there. He doesn't look like Prez, he looks so fragile and weak. I never thought I'd have to use those two words to describe him, but now they speak the truth. He has so many injuries, internal and external that his body is fighting against him. It's trying to shut down.

A shout interrupts my thoughts. I look up to see two members of Carnal arguing.

"That's so fucking disrespectful." Elle snaps.

"I don't care if you're VP, you're not ready to step up to Scalps job." Viper shouts.

"And you are?" Razor spits on the ground. "You need to respect the president, brother."

All hell breaks loose. If it hadn't been for the other Carnal members and our guys from Severed, it would have turned into a full-blown fight. I can't believe they're fighting at Scalp's funeral over who gets to take his place in the club. If they really respected him they wouldn't be arguing at all. There's a time and a place and this sure as fuck isn't it.

Angel and Ink manage to pull Razor away from Viper and the other guys hold Viper. Everyone freezes as Maggie stands in front of the fighting pair.

"You bastards!" Maggie slaps them both hard across the face. The loud crack echoing around the now silent churchyard as we all look on in shock. "Get out of my sight."

The guys drag them away in disgrace. James runs up to Maggie, squeezing her hand hard. She kneels down and whispers something in his ear. I don't know what she said but he gives her a hug. The sight makes Lucy cry and I hear Eve and Elle join her.

Maggie is starting to walk away when Angel returns. "I'm sorry you had to see that."

She shakes her head. "Don't you dare apologize for them."

"You going home?" He asks her. There's no wake for Scalp. Maggie didn't think she could handle one, so we're going to have a drink to his memory when we get back to the clubhouse instead.

"Yes, I think we're ready." She ruffles James hair as Angel gives him a cuddle.

Angel looks over at Eve and asks Maggie to wait a minute. He strolls over to us, kissing Eve on the forehead. "I'm going to go back with her, make sure she's okay. I don't like the thought of them being alone right now."

"I'll come too." Eve offers. "Might be better with both of us there."

Angel smiles weakly. "Yeah, you're right there. What about Sue, will she be okay having Elizabeth a little longer?"

"I'll let her know." I tell them. "If not, it's fine. We'll watch her for you." I gesture to Lucy to include her.

They both smile and as Angel pulls her away, Eve mouths thank you to me.

Eve

I watch Maggie as she busies herself around the kitchen. I leave Gabe and James to the game they're playing and make my way over to her.

"You don't have to do that." I let her know.

"No I do." She sniffles. "I have to keep busy."

I let her carry on. Who am I to tell her how to react to the death of the man she loves? I look over at Gabe as he plays with James. Just the possibility of him dying is such a terrifying idea; I put that out of my head straight away. It hurts too much just thinking about it so I can't imagine what pain Maggie is feeling right now.

"We're here for you, you know that right?" I let her know.

"Of course." She stops what she's doing to look at me. "You're my family. You've been more of a sister to me than my own." She looks over my shoulder and smiles. "Look at those two, you have a good man there Eve. Keep him safe."

Her voice breaks and I have to wipe my own tears. "Maggie." I say as I hold her tight.

I manage to shut the kitchen door with my foot so James doesn't have to see her like this. I know I wouldn't want Elizabeth to see me if it was the other way round.

She wipes at her eyes a few minutes later. "Sorry."

I smooth her hair from her face. "You have nothing to say apologize for."

"Eve," Maggie looks right at me. "I'm leaving."

I'm stunned. "What?"

Maggie looks around the kitchen and then out of the window, into the back garden. "So many things have happened here. So many memories.

Most of them are good ones of James growing up here. But the bad ones haunt me. The only way I was able to stay was because Scalp was here." She cries again, quickly gathering herself together. "Now he's gone, I don't want to be in this house."

"I can understand that." I let her know. "But I have the feeling you're not moving to a house nearby."

"I don't want James to grow up in this life. I've wanted to move since Rachel attacked me, but Scalp loved it here. I didn't want to make him leave, so I stayed quiet like a good wife. Now that he's gone there's nothing to stay for." She takes a deep breath. It looks like a huge weight has been lifted from her shoulders.

I know that this is the right thing for her. "Don't worry about James, you can all come and visit whenever you like. Plus, I'd love to keep in touch with Elizabeth and the rest of you of course."

I give her a tight hug. I promise to keep in touch and help her out in anyway she needs. Being an old lady makes you strong, because you have no other choice. We all have our tipping point and the death of Scalp is Maggie's. I believe that taking her and James away from all these bad memories is the right thing for them.

I'll be sad to see my friend go though. It's another loss that will be hard for us to bear.

Chapter Twenty Five

Cowboy

Lucy and I left the funeral straight after Eve and Angel. There was no reason to linger. We stopped off at Angel's to let Sue know where they'd gone. She was fine about it; she didn't need us to stay, but told us to have a drink on her to Scalp's memory.

I loved having Lucy on the back of my bike, but unfortunately the ride wasn't long and we were at the clubhouse in no time.

Now, I'm watching her talking with Dianne and Elle across the room. We've hardly spoken since 'the date' and I know that I need to apologize for my behavior. I acted like a dick and embarrassed her. At least she's fine being around me again, for that I'm thankful. Maybe now would be a good time to have a quiet talk with her.

I down what's left of my beer, making my way over to the girls. Lucy has her back to me. It's Elle who notices me first; when she does she nudges Dianne. They smile at each other and get up and leave. Confused, Lucy turns around. She looks surprised to see me standing behind her.

"Can we talk?" I ask her.

At first I think she's going to say no, but her reply surprises me. "Sure."

"In private?" I add.

Lucy looks around us then back to me. "Why?"

"Because I can't say what I need to around these pricks." I say honestly.

Her mouth turns up at the corner. "Okay."

We walk side by side as I take her to my room. I'm holding Lucy's hand in mine and it feels so natural. Neither of us says anything the whole way there.

As soon as I shut the door behind us, the words literally start to fall from of my mouth.

"I've missed you." I admit.

"I haven't been anywhere." She replies.

"No, that's not what I mean. I know you haven't been gone, but if anything that's made it worse." I try to explain. Lucy frowns, not understanding me. "I mean, it's been worse because I've seen you but you haven't been there." I try again, but just like before Lucy frowns.

"Cowboy, what are you trying to say?" She sounds confused.

I step closer, placing my hands on either side of her head. "Lucy, I've missed being your friend.

I've missed talking to you, arguing with you and just seeing you."

"I've missed that too." She whispers back.

"I'm so sorry about the way I behaved. I was a dick."

Lucy laughs. "Yeah you were."

"Well I wasn't expecting you to agree." I admit.

"Well it's the truth." She smirks.

"I've missed hearing you laugh." Lucy stops laughing and puts her hands on top of mine.

"You're forgiven." She whispers, placing a gentle kiss on my nose.

"As easy as that?" I'm shocked.

"Oh, it's not that easy. You've got a lot of making up to do." She teases.

"Oh, really?" I laugh at her.

Lucy nods her head. "I think you need to start by opening up to me."

My body stills and I remove my hands from hers. "What?"

"I'm not stupid, I know you've been through some really hard times. I think you need to talk about it. Telling me could help you."

She doesn't understand, if only it was that easy.

"I can't." The tremor in my voice is begging her not to make me do this.

"Yes you can and you will." She moves to sit on my bed, patting the space beside her.

"Come on."

"Lucy, if I tell you then you might never talk to me again." I really fucking scared of that outcome. I meant it when I told her I've missed her. Seeing so much hurt and death this year has made me realize that life is too short not to embrace it. I need to stop ignoring how I feel. I know Lucy deserves a better man than me, but I also know that I don't want her to be with anyone else. The only option I have is to stop being such a pussy and make her mine. I can't do that unless I share my demons with her, but if I do I'm scared she'll run away screaming.

Lucy

I can see that Cowboy is battling with his thoughts right now. I sit and wait for him to join me. I know he will. He has to. Holding in all the hurt isn't good for him. It's affecting all areas of his life; hell he almost killed himself because of it. I need him to open up to me if we have any chance of a future together.

Eventually Cowboy comes to sit next to me. "Tell me."

I look him straight in the eye.

"Lucy, I care about you so fucking much. I don't want to lose you." He looks so sad.

"You're not going to lose me." The pain I see in his eyes makes me want to cry.

"Trust me. When I tell you all this shit you won't want to be in my life anymore. I can't lose anyone else, Lucy." He looks so desperate. "Don't leave me."

I hold Cowboy against me. "I'm not going anywhere." I promise him.

Firstly he apologizes for the way he's treated me. He explains that he didn't like the way those guys were staring at me, or the way they were talking about me. He thought it was disrespectful.

But that's not what upsets me. What upsets me is the story he tells me about his best friend Disney and how he betrayed the club. What I hear next absolutely breaks my heart.

"I know that he betrayed the whole club. It meant more people died, but what really hurts is that he lied to me. He was my best friend, my brother!"

I hold him as he reveals more of his pain, telling me about Disney's little sister. He didn't get there in time. He blames himself for not realizing she was still alive when he walked in. He thinks it's his fault that she died. The guilt is consuming him. How could he live with this pain and not talk about it?

"Oh Cowboy." A tear falls down my face. "I'm so sorry."

He looks up at me in shock. "You're sorry?"

"Of course I am. You've endured so much pain and had to deal with it on your own." I look at him. Slowly I lean forward, placing a soft kiss on his mouth. It feels so right that I increase the pressure.

Cowboy pulls away. "You're sure?"

I nod.

Cowboy places his hands behind my head and deepens our kiss. I moan against his mouth, his lips are so soft. They fit perfectly against mine.

"God, Lucy I've wanted to kiss you for so fucking long." He growls.

"Kiss me again." I beg and he does.

With deft fingers Cowboy undoes the buttons lining the front of my dress, exposing me to his hungry gaze. He squeezes one of my breasts as he continues to kiss me. I reach for his leather cut and he helps me ease it from his shoulders.

I undo the buttons of his shirt, easing that from him as well. I'm left breathless.

Oh my fucking god!

Cowboy dressed is sexy, but Cowboy undressed is so unbelievably hot that I want to pounce on him.

He laughs, it's that deep rumble of his that I love. "Like what you see babe?"

I bite down on my lip and nod; my voice is too shaky to reply. My breath catches in my throat as he moves towards me again. Instead of sitting down next to me, he lifts me up and pulls the dress away from my body.

When he tosses it aside I'm left in my underwear and feel very vulnerable. His eyes scan me; he looks at me like he wants to devour me. The vulnerable feeling starts to fade. It's replaced with desire; he makes me feel wanted and sexy. What girl wouldn't get turned on by that?

As Cowboy places his hands on my hips his eyes are burning into me. His hands drift up, ever so slowly, caressing every inch of skin. I break out in goose bumps. By the time he reaches my breasts

I'm desperate for him to touch them, but he doesn't.

He follows my bra strap around my back. I gasp when in one deft move my bra is undone. It falls down my arms and he removes it. I'm left breathless as he stares at my hard nipples that are begging for his touch.

A groan slips from me, causing Cowboy to smirk. "You need me baby?"

"Yes." I whisper.

His expression suddenly turns serious and he takes my face in his hands. "I'm gonna take good care of you Lucy, but be patient because I've never done this before."

I'm about to ask what he's never done before, but he captures my mouth again. The way he kisses me is so sensual, so raw I know what he meant now. He's never felt like this about anyone before.

I feel it too. Nobody has ever made me feel the way Cowboy does from just a kiss.

He releases my lips, moving down to my throat. I throw my head back to allow him better access. It feels so good. Unconsciously I start to grind against him. I need more.

I hear a noise and realize it's the sound of his belt being unbuckled. I start to feel giddy inside. This is it!

He removes his dark trousers and I'm left with the delicious sight of a naked Cowboy. A commando Cowboy, who knew?

His cock looks dangerous. It's thick and long and standing to attention for me. I close the distance between us, taking his cock in my hand. Cowboy licks his fingers and teases my nipples. That feels so good.

Without thinking about it I sink down to my knees, but Cowboy stops me.

"What's wrong?" I ask him. I want to taste him.

"I don't want your mouth to be the first thing my cock sinks into." He pulls me up, before sinking to his knees in front of me. Cowboy removes my knickers, slowly teasing me by following their path with tender lips. I help him remove them by lifting my feet.

"This is what I want." He growls, placing a kiss on the top of my pussy.

In an instant he's up and lifting me in his arms. I wrap my legs around him as his kisses send me senseless. My fingers tracing lazy patterns on his back. I start to scratch the more needy I become. I want him inside me.

I whimper his name. Cowboy seems to know me so well. He understands what I need. I look into his eyes and I can see that he's nervous. He lays me down on the bed so gently. I stroke his face, trying to soothe him.

"Remember what I said Lucy." He whispers. "This is all new to me baby."

"I trust you." My heart breaks a little for this man.

I'm incapable of thought once he pushes into me. I'm lost to him. It's never felt so right with anyone else.   I understand then, this man is my soul mate.

Cowboy

I look down at Lucy as I enter her and my heart suddenly feels heavy. She holds onto my neck, looking up at me.

"I trust you." I can tell that she does, it's written all over her face.

I've never done this before. Sure I've had sex. I'm no virgin, but I've never had this kind of sex. This isn't fucking. It's making love.

When I fuck I take them on all fours, facing away from me, or reverse cowboy. It's how I earned my biker name. I don't know why, but I never wanted to see their faces, it felt too intimate for what was nothing more than satisfying an animalistic urge.

It was my favorite position until now. They never meant anything to me, but Lucy does. She means a lot to me and I know I've fallen for her. And that scares the fuck out of me.

I look into her eyes as I thrust into her. Fuck, she feels good. I can't help the satisfied groan that escapes me.

I slowly ease out and thrust back in, not speeding up, just keeping the pace, balls deep every time. The whole time I never take my eyes from her. I don't want to ever forget this moment. I want to remember the emotion in her eyes, the flush on her cheeks as she comes closer to her peak. I need to watch her face and hear her moan my name, over and over.

As I feel my own climax approaching I do something I never thought I'd ever do. I lean down, kissing her deeply as pleasure ripples through me. I love the way her nails dig into my back. I catch her gasp in a kiss as she joins me in our climax.

Another first for me is lying next to Lucy afterwards. I've never wanted anyone to share my bed. With Lucy, it's different. I never want her out of my bed.

I turn and face her, supporting myself with one arm against my head. I trace the swell of her breast with one finger. She's so responsive. I could lie like this all night, just watching her.

In that moment my fate is sealed. I know what I want. I know what I need.

"Lucy?" I say to get her attention.

"Yeah?" She looks back at me, she's drowsy and her eyes are heavy. She looks blissful though.

"Be my old lady?" I ask. I'm on edge waiting for her reply, my nerves working overtime.

"Okay." She replies sleepily.

"Really?" I ask, shocked at how easy her answer came.

"Really." She smiles back at me.

"Hell, yeah." I shout loudly. I pull my sleepy girl towards me and for the first time in my life I fall asleep spooring. It's the best night's sleep I've had in months.

Chapter Twenty Six

Cowboy

The mood in the clubhouse has been somber for the past few days. The funeral didn't help. We're all praying that Prez comes round. As we stood in that churchyard I know I for one was praying that I wouldn't be there again any time soon. I can't believe how many times we've had to visit it this year. Death seems to have taken a hold of the club. Our luck needs to change. Enough is enough.

There's a ruckus in the corner and all heads turn to see what's happening. We're a nosy bunch of fuckers.

Cherry's old lady Sam is beating him across the back of his head; I can hear the slap from over here. That must hurt. There's a chorus of laughter and a few sympathetic words of "Ouch" form some onlookers. She starts screaming at him, although I can't hear what she's saying clearly. Partly because of the speed of the words she's throwing around and because my hearing still isn't right after the explosion.

No one else looks to be stepping in and putting an end to the madness, so I make my way over to the fighting couple. Sam really has got a temper on her. What on earth has Cherry done now?

"You fucking little shit. You're a piece of scum." She screeches at him, waving a tattered piece of paper around as she shouts. "How the fuck could you do this to me? To us?" That screech is pretty painful on my ears.

"Hey, Sam." I say calmly. "What's wrong honey? What's the stupid shit done now?" She pauses from hitting him only long enough to look at me. She obviously decides hitting him is more important than answering my question because she quickly resumes her assault. Cherry places his arms over his head to try and protect himself.

"Fuck." I mutter to myself as I walk up behind her and physically lift her off Cherry. I'm sure he deserves whatever shit storm he's brought upon himself, but I can't let a brother be emasculated like this in front of the whole club. It's not on.

"Calm down and tell me what's wrong." I tell Sam firmly. She looks at me for a moment, then crumples to the seat behind her. She holds her head in her hands and starts crying. Fuck. It must be bad. Sam's a pretty tough cookie and a good old lady. I don't think I've ever seen her this upset. I shoot Cherry a glare because he must have done something really bad for her to be reacting like this.

She points her finger at Cherry. "This little shit has been dipping his wick in a Carnal whore." She sobs again. I look at Cherry in disbelief. She must be wrong. Cherry would never do that to his old lady. At least, I'm assuming he wouldn't. Sam adores him. You'd have to be blind not to see how much she loves him. I thought what they had was pretty solid. The look on Cherry's face shows the truth of Sam's words though, his guilt is plain to see. The stupid fuck.

"What the hell, Cherry?" I ask in shock.

"I can explain." Cherry stumbles over his words. I'm not sure there's anything he can say that's going to make this right. Cheating is bad enough, but with a fucking whore from Carnal? I just don't get it. If I had an old lady like Sam, I wouldn't even think about another woman, let alone act on it. I smile when I remember telling Lucy that she was my old lady now. I'd never do that to her.

"She made me feel wanted." Cherry offers. I've never heard such fucking crap come out of a brother's mouth before. "She came onto me." He offers, as though that's going to excuse the hurt he's so obviously caused Sam. I shouldn't get involved, this is between Cherry and Sam, but

Sam's a good woman and someone needs to stand up for her.

"When did this start?" I question. I mean we hardly have any contact with Carnal, so it must have been recent.

"The day of the explosion." Cherry replies, shamefaced.

"You mean the day you were supposed to be on guard and our fucking Prez got blown up!" I yell, anger flooding through my veins.

"She... she..." Cherry can't get his words out.

"Let me guess?" Sam spits out. "She gave you a fucking blow job and you couldn't say no to her."

Cherry's face shows that Sam was on the mark.

"So let me repeat my question, Cherry." I say calmly. I'm barely restraining my anger as it all suddenly becomes clear to me. Right now I'd like nothing more than to punch him to the floor. "You were on guard. Instead of watching our backs you were getting your fucking dick sucked? And because you were thinking with your fucking cock instead of your head you missed someone walking into Carnal and throwing grenades in the fucking clubhouse?" My voice has risen with every word and brought attention from several other members who are now standing around cursing.

"I didn't know." Cherry pleads. "Honest Cowboy, if I could swap places with Prez right now I would." Cherry sounds broken.

"This isn't the time for this. We'll deal with this around the table when Prez is back." I'm so angry right now I could throw him across the room. You never let your brothers down. *Never.*

"Get out of my sight. Now!" I yell. Cherry scurries from the room, head down and not looking anyone in the eye as he leaves.

"Come here, Sam." I draw the sobbing woman into my arms.

My mind's working overtime. It's too much of a coincidence that Cherry has some whore offer to blow him off at exactly the same time the Carnal clubhouse was attacked. This needs looking into.

Chapter Twenty Seven

Cowboy

There's still no news from the hospital about Prez, so for now Angel is taking care of the day-to-day running of the club. I've unofficially become his right hand man. I have a lot more respect for his role as VP now. I didn't realize how hard he had to work.

The intercom from the gate buzzes. "Angel, Declan from the pub is here to see you." Ice shouts as he looks at the camera feed.

"Buzz him in." Angel tells him as he strides across the room to the front door. Ice and I join him to greet our guest. A week ago I'd never have thought we'd be seeing Declan walk through these doors.

Declan looks tired when he walks in. He's obviously not been to bed at all judging from the shadows under his eyes and the scruffy looking stubble on his chin.

"You okay?" I ask him.

"Yeah. Long night." He sighs in reply. "You got somewhere where we can talk?" He takes in the bar and the lounge area and smiles.

I roll my eyes. "Yeah, yeah. Not as posh as your place. I get it."

Angel laughs. "Follow me." Angel leads him to Prez's office and indicates for Ink and I to join them.

Declan sinks gratefully into the leather sofa against the wall and accepts the shot of whisky Angel has poured for him. We wait till he's taken a mouthful before jumping in and harassing him.

"What."

"Have you heard…"

"Any news…"

We all speak at once. Angel silences Ink and me with a look. He's the acting president and should be the one leading this conversation.

Declan laughs at us all, wiping a hand across his tired eyes.

"Give me a moment guys. I've got some news you'll want to hear. It's just been a long drive." He takes another mouthful of whisky then starts his story.

"I've been in the city with some contacts of mine." He offers. "These guys have been looking into this drug problem for me." He pauses as a huge yawn takes over The guy really does look wrecked.

"I called in a few favors that I was owed and I think I know who's behind it." I'm about to interrupt when he stalls me with his hand. "I also think I know where they're storing the stuff."

Wow. This guy really does have some useful contacts. We've not been able to find anything out from our sources. It makes me wonder just what he used to do in the past to be this connected to these kind of people.

"It's a new firm from the city. They've decided to spread out and make a name for themselves. They're well funded, but greedy. That's why the drugs they're selling are poor quality. They don't give a fuck about the addicts it will kill, just about moving the stuff and making money. The way I understand it is that they deal for a few months then move in and offer protection services to the businesses that are affected by the crime that the drug wave creates."

This is serious shit. I can see it on everyone's faces.

"We're not used to dealing with organized criminals. I'm not sure that even working with Carnal we'll have the resources to fight it." Angel sounds disappointed. He's right. There's no way we can take on an organization like this.

"I might be able to help you there." Declan offers. "Let's just say my contacts still owe me quite a few favors and I'm prepared to call them in to keep this place safe."

"Why would you do that?" Ink asks, distrust in his voice.

"I told you guys I needed a change of scenery. Severed is that change and it's in my best interests to help keep it safe." He sounds pretty genuine.

"So where did you get contacts that can help with this shit?" Angel questions him.

"That's my past and it's staying in the past." Declan's firm in his response. "All you need to know is that I have them and they're going to help."

"You're asking me to take a lot on trust." Angel doesn't sound convinced.

"I know." Declan offers. "Have I done or said anything to you guys that would make you doubt me?" He doesn't sound offended. He understands our concern and that's reassuring in itself.

"I guess I'm going to have to trust you on this one." Angel replies. It's not easy for us accepting outside help, especially when we don't know where it's coming from, but we don't really have any other choice.

"Oh, I had it confirmed that it was these guys that blew up the Carnal clubhouse. It was in revenge for Carnal killing their dealer."

He's confirmed what we already suspected.

"We're going to have to involve Carnal in that case." Angel speaks slowly. "I'd rather not considering the infighting they've got going on at the moment, but this affects them as much as us."

"Are you sure VP?" Ink voices the question before I can. "The way they're fighting each other I'm not sure that's such a good idea right now."

"I think I have to." Angel sounds resigned. "I'll call Razor and let him know what we found out, but suggest he lets us handle it for now. At the moment we still don't have a location, we can let them know when we need the manpower."

Angel is VP for a reason. He's more calm and level headed than either Ink or me. We'd have played this one close to our chests, but he's right. Now isn't the time to keep Carnal in the dark. If it was the other way round and we'd just lost our president we'd want to know anything and everything.

I still for a moment at the realization that we could still lose our own president. There's no more news from the hospital on Prez. He's stable and in a coma. Teresa's spending most of her time at his bedside and our old ladies are taking it in turns to sit with her.

"I need to get back and get some sleep." Declan rises slowly from the sofa. "It's been a long ass night." He groans.

"Thank you." Angel gently slaps him on the back. "We appreciate your support on this."

"Anytime." Declan throws over his shoulder as he leaves the room.

The three of us look at each other. This is probably the toughest thing we've had to face as a club.

Chapter Twenty Eight

Lucy

All morning at work I've had Cowboy on my mind. I've found myself daydreaming about him far too much and that's not good when you've got customers to serve. Last night was amazing. ! I never suspected that when Cowboy asked to talk to me in private that it would turn out the way it did. But I'm not complaining. I've still got a stupid grin on my face.

Cowboy was so caring; from the way he held me, making love to me so gently and then later when he woke me up with his kisses. He made sure that I was satisfied. Trust me, I was very satisfied and more than once. I guess I expected something different from a tough alpha guy like him, I thought he would be more focused on his own release than mine.

This morning felt strange, but not awkward. It felt off because it felt so right, if that makes any sense. I still can't believe he asked me to be his old lady. I thought I'd dreamed it until he reminded me earlier. The way I understand it that's a pretty big commitment from a biker, it's almost as big as getting married.

The rational part of me tells me that this is all happening too quickly, but the sexually sated part of me tells me to just go for it and embrace it. There's a connection between us that is more than just sex. The fact that Cowboy recognized that as well is what has me so surprised I think.

I haven't seen the girls yet, but they'll all know by now. Elle spotted me trying to sneak out of Cowboy's room when I left for work this morning. It won't have been hard for her to work out what went down last night. I know I'll never hear the last of it and that's before they've heard the best part of it all. I can't wait to see their faces when I tell them about being an old lady.

I pretended not to see Elle as I was already pushing it for time. My mobile phone is suffering for it now though. She's been blowing it up with texts all morning.

I look up when I hear the front door open to see a really tired looking Declan entering the bar.

He sees me staring and shakes his head. "Yeah I know. I look like shit." He sounds exhausted, but still manages a smile for me.

"I wasn't going to say that." I quickly answer. He just gives me a knowing look.

"But you were thinking it." He smirks.

I laugh at him because he's right. He really does look like shit.

"I'm gonna go up to bed. I don't think I can stay awake another minute." He groans as he makes his way to the door to his apartment above the bar.

"No problem." I answer, turning to attend to a couple that want to pay their lunch bill.

"Michelle arrives for her shift before you leave today right?" He sounds unsure. That surprises me. Declan must be tired, he normally knows everyone's shifts off the top of his head.

"Yeah, why?"

"Ask her to lock up for me. I've a feeling I won't be waking up until tomorrow."

"Okay." I laugh as I watch him go. Poor guy.

Two hours later Michelle arrives signaling the end of my shift. She agrees to lock up and I'm out of here. I've never been so grateful to see the end of my shift. I've spent far too much of it thinking about Cowboy and what I'd like to do to him. I hadn't realized I was capable of such impure thoughts. I like it.

When I arrive home I quickly shed my work clothes and bask in a long, hot shower before slipping on a light maxi dress. It's feels good. I welcome the loose fit as my shorts had been digging into my stomach all through my shift.

I collapse onto the sofa and replay the memories from last night. I can't help grinning to myself. It was so good and I want more. I need Cowboy. My decision made I grab my car keys and head off to find him.

As I drive to the clubhouse I find myself giggling like a schoolgirl because of the way I'm feeling. I'm on my way to see my new boyfriend, but this is different. This is much more serious than some teenage crush.

Recognizing my car the prospects open the gate for me.

"Hey Lucy" One of them greets me as I exit my car.

"Hi." I smile back.

"Here to see the girls?" He asks.

My cheeks burn. "Erm, no Cowboy."

His eyebrows rise at the obvious blush on my cheeks.

"Right." I try to scurry away. "He's in the gym!" He shouts after me.

I throw my hand over my head, gesturing my thanks and head in the direction of the gym. Why am I behaving like this? I'm a grown woman, there's no reason for me to be embarrassed.

I can hear a smacking noise, as I get closer to the clubs gym, followed by a groaning sound. I quietly open the door and stand there eyes wide at the sight before me. Standing in the far corner of the room is one very hot and sweaty looking Cowboy. He's beating the hell out of a punch bag. His body is slick and shiny with sweat and his muscles are swollen.

I bite down on my lip. God he looks so hot. He growls and groans as his punches become harder and faster I can feel myself starting to get worked up.

"If you don't get in here soon I'll have to drag you in." He shouts over to me as he continues to pound on the bag.

I look around to see if there's anyone around. I feel myself blush at being caught spying on him.

Before I have time to move Cowboy stops punching and storms over to me. It's an imposing sight. It's only because I know the real Cowboy that I'm not quivering with fear at him right now.

He pulls me into the room, locking the door behind us. I look nervously at the locked door. What's he got planned?

Cowboy places his arms around my waist and lifts me over his shoulder. I squeal in surprise, which earns me a smack on the ass. He moves us across the room and when he places me back down, we're behind the weights.

"God, I've missed you." He kisses me deeply.

"Mmm," I return his kiss. "I've missed you too."

"Fucking love this dress." He growls. "Makes this so easy."

A moment later my dress is lifted over my head and my underwear's discarded. I don't dare complain. Not that I'd want to. He's teasing my clit and I really don't want him to stop. "Oh God." I moan. "I've been thinking about you all day."

"Me too." He's only wearing tiny black shorts and as he pulls them down and frees his cock I find my mouth watering. "Ready baby?"

He doesn't give me time to say yes before he's thrusting inside me. This is so different to last night and this morning when he was gentle with me. This's primal fucking. I throw my head back in pleasure and hit the wall, but I don't complain. I don't want Cowboy to stop because this is exactly what I craved.

When we've both reached our release he lets me back down gently. I almost can't stand as my legs are like jelly after that.

"God that was fucking amazing." He grins. He helps me dress. His actions are so tender they're in complete contrast to how he was treating me just a few moments ago.

I have a silly grin on my face and he looks at me as if to ask why.

"You may be a bad ass biker Cowboy," I grin at him, 'but deep down you're a big teddy bear. My teddy bear" I giggle. Shit. I hope I haven't offended him. I suspect the last thing a tough biker would want to be compared to is a cuddly toy. I needn't have worried.

"I don't know about teddy bear babe." He grins back wickedly. "I might accept grizzly bear." He laughs.

Right now standing in this gym I think I'm the happiest I've ever been. I look at the man in front of me. He's fucking gorgeous, he's badass and he's broken. But he's mine.

He leads us back to his room where he proceeds to spend the rest of the night showing me how badass he is.

Chapter Twenty Nine

Cowboy

I had to force myself out of bed this morning. I didn't want to let Lucy go, but she's at work and I had to get up for this meeting. It's with Carnal and Declan. It's an important meeting so I need to get Lucy out of my mind. I need to concentrate. That's harder than I thought it would be as memories of our lovemaking keep coming back to me.

"Alright, let's start this thing." Angel begins. He doesn't call the meeting to order in the traditional way with the gavel and I understand. Prez still hasn't come out of his coma, but he's still our president and it just doesn't feel right holding a meeting without him at the head of the table, even though Angel is legitimately taking his place for now.

"Declan, these are the guys from Carnal." Angel introduces everyone. Viper and Razor are here with a couple of other guys and Ink, Cherry and I are here for Severed. We're not bringing this to the whole club. From what Declan told us yesterday we need to keep it down to a small, tight group.

"Can we trust him?" Viper looks at Declan with suspicion. He's the loose cannon in the room. He's got a hair trigger temper. I guess he's finding it hard being on the same side as Severed, without us adding a third party into the mix as well.

"Definitely." Angel assures him and to their credit, the guys from Carnal accept his word. The two clubs have come a long way since Satan died.

I understand their reservations about including Declan in this meeting. I respect them for trusting Angel's word that he's okay.

"I asked you to come," Angel speaks directly to the Carnal guys, "because Declan has some information for us."

Only Ange knows what the news is. He called the meeting early this morning straight after receiving a call from Declan at breakfast.

"I'll fill you all in at the meeting." He'd told us when Ink asked what it was.

The speed at which the meeting was put together tells me that this new information is important.

Declan nods at us all. "Thank you all for letting me be here, I know you guys don't normally let outsiders in and I respect that." We all nod our heads in acknowledgement. "As some of you may know I'd reached out to some contacts of mine and they got back to me early this morning.

They've found out who these guys are and more importantly, where they're storing the drugs."

"So who are they?" Razor interrupts. He's only asking the question that's burning at the back of all our minds.

"They're a new organized gang who are starting out with us smaller towns to make some money." He tells us. They need to get their processes up and running before they make a run on some of the bigger gangs in the city.

Razor looks up to the ceiling. "Fuck. So you're telling me we're fucking guinea pigs for these guys?"

We all know that when the word organized comes in to play its serious. There's a huge difference between a gang and an organized gang. They have the resources and networks to be very fucking dangerous.

"Carry on Declan." Angel looks tense, we all are. You could cut the atmosphere in here with a knife.

"This morning I got the call telling me where they're storing and packing the drugs." Declan looks around the room, making sure we're all paying attention.

I'm relieved now that we involved Declan. I dread to think how long it would have taken us without his help. The delay would have led to more deaths. I'm not naïve. Whatever course of action we choose to follow now will result in deaths. It's inevitable, especially with the hand fate has been dealing us. I look around the room wondering which of us won't survive whatever action we're about to embark on.

"So lets go." Viper stands, his chair falling to the floor.

"Sit down." Razor snaps.

"Fuck that! Lets do this!" Vipers almost jumping up and down, rage flowing through his veins. He's itching for a fight. Looking at the resigned faces around the room he's the only one who is.

"Sit down." Razor grinds out, "We can't just go running in there like fucking idiots!" His dislike for his fellow club member is obvious. I just hope their personal battle for their club doesn't fuck up us all working together.

Viper looks around the room in disgust before putting his chair right and taking his seat.

"We'll do this properly. We can't go rushing in there without a plan." Angel looks around as we nod our understanding.

I smirk over at Viper in a fuck you gesture. See that asshole? That's how we've survived and your MC is always in the shit.

"I can help." Declan adds. "I have the manpower and weapons for you. From our surveillance there's a large number of them and they're well armed. You'll need all the help you can get. We're going to have to go in stealthily under cover of night if we have a chance of catching them by surprise. My guys are trained for this type of combat."

"That sounds like a plan." Angel accepts his offer for us all. There are no smiles around the room, other than Viper. This is serious shit, Frankly none of us are experienced enough to handle it.

I thank god that we have Declan on our side. I'm starting to have a lot of respect for the guy. Whatever secret shit he has hidden in his past is working out in our favor. I'm grateful. When he's ready to share it with us, I'm sure he will. Until then I'm just going to be very fucking thankful he's here.

Chapter Thirty

Cowboy

The mood is still somber in the clubhouse after the meeting with Carnal and Declan. Shit's getting real now. In just a matter of hours we're going to war against an unknown enemy. At least when we were fighting Satan we had a rough idea of the hell that we were up against.

Part of me just wants this to be over. The other part of me is anxious about what's ahead. A few weeks ago when I was ready to end my life I'd have happily rushed in tonight all guns blazing. But I have Lucy now. I can't do that to her. I need to watch my back. Selfishly I now want more time. I want to spend a long life with Lucy. I hope to fuck the click of that empty chamber was Fate's way of telling me she's not ready for me yet. That I'm going to get some more time to try and find some happiness with Lucy.

There's a commotion in the corner of the room and I sigh when I see that it's Cherry and his old lady Sam again. What's the stupid fuck done to upset her now? I decide to head over as Cherry looks pretty heated and I want to make sure Sam's okay.

"How could you do that to her? She fucking loved me!" Cherry wails at Sam. What the fuck is he on about? Who loved him?

"I told you, it wasn't me, Cherry. I swear." Sam has tears in her eyes. I'm not sure how long this argument has been going on before I became aware of it, but from the state of Sam I'm guessing a while.

"She killed Kirsty." Cherry looks at Sam with such pain in his eyes.

"Wait." I hold up my hands. "Who the fuck is Kirsty and how could Sam have anything to do with killing anyone?" I ask.

"Kirsty is the whore from Carnal." Sam cries even more now. "Turns out Cherry here has been seeing her behind my back. I guess one quick blowjob wasn't enough for him and now the stupid cow has taken a drug overdose and he thinks I had something to do with it." Sam is really distraught, so much so that when I offer her my arms she sinks face first into my chest. Her tears quickly soak through my thin shirt. Cherry is a fucking idiot.

"You mean that stupid whore you were getting a blow job from when you were supposed to be guarding the bikes?" I hiss at Cherry over Sam's head.

Cherry takes offense at me calling her a whore and moves to hit me. He doesn't see Ink standing behind him and his blow is cut short when Ink grabs him by the arms and restrains him. What the fuck is happening here?

"I loved her." Cherry shouts. "Don't you dare call her a whore."

"You love Sam." I correct him. Cherry and Sam are solid, or I thought they were.

"Kirsty loved me, she made me feel special." Cherry insists his fist now on his heart. "Sam's not even interested in me any more." I'm not surprised, not after finding out he had his cock sucked by a fucking whore.

"Fucking idiot." Ink joins in. "Did it not occur to you that the fucking whore was paid to distract you so they could get in with their fucking grenades?" Ink asks in disbelief.

"No, she loved me." Cherry persists, although this time there's a little less certainty in his voice. Why can't he see what's staring us all in the face here but him.

The whore was paid to distract him. I suspect she was paid in drugs hence her overdosing. The cynic in me thinks the drugs were deliberately tampered with to leave no witnesses.

"One blow job and you think she loves you?" Ink laughs at Cherry. There's derision in his voice.

"Tell them." Sam manages to spit out from where she's hiding on my chest still. "Tell them how many times you went back for more."

"You did what?" Ink and I say at the same time, disbelief in our voices.

"She loved me." Cherry offers, even more weakly than before. I don't recognize him, he's so pathetic and weak right now.

"Trust me brother, a blow job never has and never will equal love when it comes from a fucking whore." Ink advises him.

"I can't believe you were that stupid, Cherry." I'm almost lost for words at his stupidity. I've known him for a lot of years, I know he had a bad childhood and that left him feeling insecure, but I thought he was over that. Sam loves him, anyone can see it. Why he'd want to go off with a fucking whore when he has Sam at home is beyond me.

"She must have been a better actress than she was a whore is all I can say." Ink mutters. "Face up to it. You were used mate."

I can see Ink wants to say more, but he's biting his tongue. I'm in the same position. I want to lay into Cherry right now for his stupidity. The same stupidity that let someone get past him into the compound and blow that clubhouse up. It's his fault that Scalp is dead and our Prez is still in a coma. The only reason I don't hit him is that they got past the Carnal guards as well.

"You need to wake up and realize what you've got mate." I tell him instead. "Or what you did have." I shake my head and motion to Sam. "She loves you and fuck knows why. She deserves better than some stupid fucked up guy who would choose a whore over her." I've got a bitter taste in my mouth and suddenly I want nothing more than to smash his face in.

"If I were you I'd get out of my sight." I spit at him. "Now!"

Cherry obviously sees the anger in my eyes. When Ink releases him from his hold he rushes from the room.

I motion to Diane who has been watching from the sidelines and ask her to take Sam away and make sure she's all right.

"We can't do this if we're not together." Ink sighs. He's right. We're about to head into hell. We won't survive it if we don't have each other's backs. I think we need to ask Angel to let Cherry sit this one out, the fucker isn't thinking clearly that's for sure.

Chapter Thirty One

Cowboy

It's one of those perfect nights where it's so clear you can see every star in the sky. That means it's not a good night for launching an assault on a drug warehouse. There's too much visibility out here and the bright, full moon taunts us with its brilliance.

We reach the hill where we've agreed to meet the rest of the team. The Carnal guys are antsy. They're still hurting after losing their leader. It's too soon for them to have put their dislike of each other aside and voted in a new president. Razor has a loose rein over them for the time being as VP, but I'm not sure he'll win against Viper. He's a formidable opponent. I just hope they don't let their own problems get in the way of what we're trying to do tonight. This is going to be difficult enough as it is. I'm also concerned that Viper isn't a team player.

I'm not sure what the hell Declan used to do in his past life, but it's clear he knows what he's talking about. He also has some pretty impressive contacts, so he's taking command. It feels wrong for us to be accepting orders from an outsider, but we've got to look at the bigger picture here. Not to mention he has some serious firepower with him. Looking closer I can see it's all military standard, that shit looks scary. The guys he's brought with him all look like military as well. They're very tight lipped though. In fact they only speak in direct response to a question or command from Declan. The way they work so closely together tells me they've known each other for quite some time. I have a new respect for Declan. He's a fucking badass.

The building ahead of us looks almost derelict but from the surveillance Declan's team carried out it's very far from that inside. The exterior has been left alone to help disguise the true purpose of what's being stored in there.

The upper level has a fallen roof on one corner and the moonlight shows through the broken panes of glass straight to the other side. They don't have anything stored up there. Intel tells us everything is in the center of the ground floor.

Declan advises us that the latest recon shows at least thirty guards around and in the building. Stealth is going to be the only way to accomplish our plan this evening. I'd sigh out loud if I could get away with it. Stealth and MC clubs aren't really partners in crime, especially Carnal MC. They're more likely to go storming in kicking and screaming.

Declan's guys are going to go in first and clear a perimeter for us. We'll follow in after with Declan and the guys from Carnal.

There are more of the enemy than there are of us, but Declan assures us that won't be a problem. Let's hope our lack of combat experience won't be a problem either.

The approach to the building is by one long dirt road. The rough ground around that has been set with trip wires and sensors. The security here is high tech and expensive. I wish we could afford a fraction of this back at the clubhouse. It also tells me these guys inside know their shit and I'd be a fool if that didn't worry me.

Within moments of moving ahead the front team signal it's okay for us to come forward. I'm crawling along on my belly and wondering how the hell I got here. All I ever wanted was a quiet life and to be left alone to ride my bike. Joining Severed MC had given me that until this last year.

I've seen more shit and death and horror this last year than most people ever have to suffer in a lifetime. Karma sure is a bitch. I just wish I knew what I'd done to piss her off so badly. I'd gladly make amends.

By the time we make it inside the warehouse it's clear that Declan's guys have done most of the work. We edge cautiously nearer to the main room in the center of the building, but each corner we turn and each door we open is clear.

When I reach the main area inside the warehouse I draw in a deep breath.

Holy fuck!

I'm no banker but even I can tell that I'm staring at millions of dollars of drugs in front of me. In one corner of the room a group of terrified workers are kneeling on the floor, hands behind their bowed heads as one of Declan's guys' covers them with a gun. The poor fuckers look half starved to me. They're wearing just the skimpiest underwear, ensuring there's nowhere for them to secrete any of the precious product they've been weighing and packing.

The scale of the operation astounds me. Declan told us that no matter how organized and dangerous these guys appear, they're pretty new on the scene and small fry compared to most. They're trying to carve out a place for themselves. If this is small I'd hate to see what anything more serious looks like. The only advantage we have is that the bigger organizations aren't likely to retaliate, as they'll be glad to get rid of them.

The inside of the room is clinically clean, huge white spotlights against the stark white walls almost blinding us. There are long trestles across the length of the room, which are covered in an assortment of chemicals. I'm not sure what most of them are but I do recognize antifreeze. *Fuck*!

They're mixing some serious shit into these drugs. Declan told us that they mix the drugs with other stuff to make it go further. The purer the drug the more lethal it is, unless they're mixing it with poisonous substances like these fuckers clearly are.

In the center of the room there's a guy already tied to a chair, a black bag over his head. There are at least three of Declan's guys covering him. I'm guessing this makes him one of the leaders.

Declan comes over to us, he's covered in a mixture of blood and dirt.

"We've got it under control here. It might be better if you guys get out of here and let us finish it off." He whispers, looking back at the man tied to the chair. "Plausible deniability and all that." He smirks.

Shit. In this setting and carrying that gun Declan looks like one scary motherfucker. Nothing like the friendly bar owner I've come to know.

"You sure?" Angel asks quietly. I can hear the relief in his voice. We're all out of our comfort zone here.

"Yeah. We've got it covered." Declan responds. "You guys head home."

"Not so fast." Viper interrupts. "Is that the fucker that ordered the hit on our clubhouse?" He indicates to the guy on the chair.

"One of them." Declan confirms.

Viper wastes no time in striding over and putting a bullet in the center of the black hood, between the mans eyes I assume.

"Fuck." Declan hisses. It all happened so quickly no one had chance to stop Viper. "We needed to get some more info out of him."

Viper, idiot that he is, is oblivious to the damage he's just done. He stands there in front of the body with a shit-eating smile on his face. I almost can't believe my eyes when he opens his jeans and urinates over the dead guy.

I have to turn away, I can't watch this shit. "Jesus." I mutter.

"Fucking hell." Angel growls.

"That's for Scalp you fucker." He grins maniacally.

Everyone in the room, including the guys from his own club, look disgusted.

Declan just mutters "Amateurs" under his breath. What the hell did this guy used to do?

Reassured that Declan no longer needs us, Angel agrees we'll head back to the clubhouse. Razor seems to have calmed Viper down a little and they agree to let Declan deal with everything, although Viper looks a little upset when he's told the drugs are to be destroyed. That's Carnal for you. It would be a shame if Viper became president as he'll return Carnal back to the way it was when Satan was alive. All Scalp's hard work would be undone.

All appears to be going well and we start to leave, that is until a guy rushes into the room waving a gun in the air and shooting wildly. Declan looks surprised, but reacts quickly, stopping him in his stride with a single bullet.

"Aw fuck!" Angel groans. He stares at me, his eyes wide and I don't understand why.

Then I feel it. Declan wasn't quick enough. There's a burning sensation and my vision starts to blur. I move my hand to where I feel the pain and it comes away covered in blood. My legs go weak and as I sink to the floor in slow motion I hear Angel screaming my name. Then everything goes black.

Chapter Thirty Two

Lucy

I wait as patiently as I can, but I'm not making a good job of it. I keep pacing and sitting and then I stand again to repeat the whole thing. My eyes remain fixed on the front door and nothing else. I don't even notice Cherry when he comes to see if I've heard anything.

"Lucy?" His voice startles me and I jump in my seat.

"Cherry?" I look up at him.

"Yeah babe, you okay? I've been trying to talk to you for the past five minutes.

"Sorry." I answer abruptly, my eyes returning to focus on the door.

"Any news?" He asks.

"No." I snap, still not taking my eyes away from the door. I'm scared that if I do I might miss something.

"You okay darling?" Is he really that stupid?

No I'm not okay. I'm living my worst nightmare, sitting here praying to God that it's not true. Of course I don't tell him that, it would mean moving my attention from the door. Instead I just nod my head. I think he gets the point as he leaves. I think he's left anyway as I don't hear him anymore. I can't take my eyes away from that door.

My thoughts turn to what's happening on the other side of the door. I'm shaking from nerves and my stomach is churning. I feel sick with dread.

Cowboy asked me to wait for him at the clubhouse while he went out on business. When I heard the loud noises outside I knew something was wrong. Doc came running in closely followed by Angel and Ink who were carrying an unconscious Cowboy. They were all covered in blood.

I screamed at them to tell me what had happened, but nobody spoke. It's as though I was invisible. They were more concerned about getting Cowboy into Doc's makeshift hospital room. It's packed with the latest medical kit and really looks like it belongs in a hospital. It's a sign of the troubled times the club has had to endure that they felt the need to create this room.

I followed them of course, tears pouring down my face. As soon as they laid him down on the bed Doc ordered us all out. Angel and Ink led me from the room, but not before I'd stared down at a deathly pale Cowboy who looked lifeless on the bed.

Shutting the door behind us they told me I couldn't enter. They didn't stay around though, they were anxious to see Eve and Elle and let them know they were okay. I don't blame them. I'm sure they'll come back as soon as they've reassured the girls. That's their best friend in there after all. I hold in a sob knowing it's also my future in there.

So here I am, waiting for news of Cowboy. I'm imagining all sorts of outcomes and none of them have a happy ending.

I jump at the sound of the door opening, quickly rising to my feet as Doc appears. He doesn't say anything to me. He just smiles at me and I don't like it. It's an 'I'm sorry' kind of smile.

"Where's Angel?" He asks.

"I don't know." I answer hesitantly.

He just nods and walks away, leaving me standing in front of the open door. I don't miss the bloodstains all over his clothes though.

I take a very deep breath to try and steady my nerves, but it does nothing to help me.

I walk into the room, stand still at the side of the bed and look down on him. I'm struggling to hold back my tears as I look at him lying there, so pale and still. The realization hits me then and I fall into the chair at the side of the bed.

"Oh God." I cry. He's left me; he's really left me!

I stare at his lifeless body, angry tears now streaming down my face. I don't know how I'm going to cope. Cowboy became such a huge part of my life without me even realizing it and now he's been ripped away from me, just as we had our chance at happiness.

"Don't leave me." I beg taking a hold of his hand and squeezing it.

I cry even harder when he doesn't return the squeeze like he usually would. This isn't fair. We only had such a short time together.

"I loved you." I sob, resting my head on his chest, ignoring the blood. "I loved you so fucking much and now you've left me."

"Lucy?" I look up and see Doc at the door, Angel is at his side and they're both staring at me.

"What's the matter, babe?" Angel asks. He looks a little scared to come any closer. I must look a real mess.

I cry harder, standing up to answer him. "Oh Angel, I can't believe he's gone!"

"What?" He sounds shocked. I must have broken the news to him before Doc could.

"He's dead." I cry. "I can't believe he's left me."

I almost collapse to the floor but Angel is quickly at my side, holding me up.

"Lucy," Doc begins. "He's not dead"

I still, halting my sobbing. "But, look at him."

"Lucy," Doc smiles. "Cowboy's not dead."

"What?" I look from Doc to Cowboy. Why is he making such a cruel joke?

"Oh babe, I'm sorry I didn't explain before I left to find Angel." Doc moves closer and Angel steps aside to allow him to stand next to me. "I had to find Angel, asked me to find him straight away when I was done. Cowboy isn't dead; he's just heavily sedated. I'll bet he's coming around and can hear everything that's going on." He laughs.

"I'm sorry." Angel places a hand on my shoulder. "I should have asked Doc to make sure you were the first to know. I still can't get my head around you being his old lady."

I look Angel in the eye. His words have started to warm the chill around my heart. I am Cowboy's old lady. I grin widely. Angel smiles at me and Doc giggles.

"You hear that you lucky bastard," he says as he leans closer to Cowboy. "Survived a shoot out and got yourself an old lady all in the space of a week."

A shoot out? No wonder they're all covered in dirt and blood.

"So, he's going to be okay?" I ask Doc.

"He'll be sore for a while, but yes, he'll be okay." Doc confirms. "The bullet went straight through his arm. It looked a lot worse than it was."

"Lucky sod has you to care for him and help get him better." Angel teases, but I'm not in the mood for joking right now. I'm still suffering shock from thinking he'd died.

"We'll give you some time alone." Doc indicates for Ange to exit the room with him. "Be careful touching his stomach and left arm." He warns me as they both leave.

As soon as they've gone I bury my face in Cowboy's neck and breathe his scent in.

"God, I'm so relieved you're going to be okay." I place a kiss on his lips and am sure I hear a groan. "Cowboy?"

Another groan and I jump up; checking over his body to make sure I haven't hurt him.

"Lucy?" He whispers, his voice croaky and weak. My heart jumps in relief.

"Cowboy?" I smile for the first time since I saw him being carried in here.

I see him struggle to talk. "Shh, just relax."

"I heard you." He coughs. "You love me."

I actually laugh. "Yes, I do." I reassure him.

"I love you too." He whispers. Oh my god I could cry right now. "My old lady." He adds.

Tears slide down my cheeks and I don't bother wiping them away.

"Seeing as I'm your old lady now don't you think I should know your real name." I know this isn't really the time to ask him, but it's been killing me not knowing. I hate calling him Cowboy all the time.

"Ash." He answers me in a quiet growl. "But only you get to call me that."

"Deal." I kiss him hard then. I'm so relieved. "I love you Ash." I whisper.

Chapter Thirty Three

Cowboy

Thank fuck Doc has finally let me out of that makeshift hospital of his. My arm is stinging like a bitch, but I'll live. I can't do with being ill. Lucy's snuggled up at the side of me on my good side. She's quiet. I think she's still coming to terms with thinking she'd lost me. The pain in her voice when she thought I was dead will always haunt me. I vow to myself to make it up to her, to always put a smile on her face. I never want to hear her hurting like that again.

I reach down and draw her face to mine so I can kiss her. It's gentle and tender and generates a series of whoops and cheers from the other members in the clubhouse lounge. Lucy flushes with embarrassment. Fuck, I love the blush in her cheeks, it shows her innocence. She's not so

innocent in the bedroom though and I'm tempted to take her back there to show her how I really feel.

We're interrupted by the arrival of Teresa. She must be taking a break from the hospital. It's hard on us all spending time with Prez when he's unconscious. She looks absolutely exhausted. All this stress can't be doing her any good, especially this late in her pregnancy. She's only got another month or so to go.

She sinks heavily into the seat at my side. "Hey, Cowboy." She greets me with tired eyes and a weary voice. She's so exhausted she only manages a smile in greeting to Lucy. I'm worried about her, this isn't the Teresa we know and love.

Sue walks over to join us. It looks like she's been crying. "What's wrong, Sue?" Lucy asks, concerned.

"Nothing darlin'." Sue smiles. "Everything's right." She's clutching an envelope to her chest and looks the most peaceful I've seen her since her attack.

"What's happened?" I ask.

Sue doesn't answer; instead she passes me the envelope. I take out the single sheet of notepaper inside and peruse the neat handwriting.

Sue,

I understand that this belongs to you and I wanted to return it. I know how much this means to you. I hope it brings you some peace.

Your friend

Declan

X

That's all that was in the envelope so I look to Sue for an explanation. She pulls open the neck of the shirt she's wearing to reveal a mans ring resting on the end of a gold chain.

"He's found Elvis's ring for me." Lucy gasps at the same time Teresa lets out a little cry. Fuck. It even makes me feel soft for a moment. "I've put it on a chain as I don't want to risk ever losing it again."

She moves to sit next to Teresa who pulls her into a hug. It's not been a year yet and their shared loss still hits them deeply. I know Prez said Teresa was really upset her Dad wouldn't get to see their new baby. This should be an exciting time for them both; instead Teresa's grieving for her father and still doesn't know if her husband will survive. No one deserves that.

My phone rings. When I look at the display its Angel. "Is Teresa with you?" he asks. He sounds serious.

"Yeah, what's up? You're at the hospital with Prez aren't you?" I question.

"I need to talk to Teresa." He responds abruptly. Shit. No. I don't want to hand her phone, but I do with a shaking hand.

"Teresa, honey, its Angel for you." She's about to thank me when she sees the look in my eyes. Hesitantly she reaches for the phone. Dread written across her face as she greets Angel. I can't hear what he's saying on the other end of the phone, but her face says it all.

Teresa goes white as a sheet and a tear escapes her eye. "Oh God." She exclaims. "No. I don't believe it." She gasps out the last words. "I should have been there." She wails.

Suddenly her face changes from shocked to puzzled. It's only there for a moment when she starts to cry heavily, dropping the still open phone from her hand.

Chapter Thirty Four

Cowboy

I don't know whether to comfort Teresa or reach for the phone and talk to Angel. I choose the phone, hoping that Lucy and Sue can take care of her.

"Angel? It's me. Teresa's not doing so well." I let him know.

"What do you mean?" He asks. I can hear the surprise in his voice.

"What did you expect?" How did he not expect her to react badly to news like that.

"I thought she'd be elated." He pauses. "I knew she'd be pissed he woke up when she wasn't here, but I didn't think she'd be upset." He finishes.

What the fuck?

"He's not dead?" I don't understand it. I was convinced he'd rung to tell her that Prez had gone, especially when she reacted like that. Lucy and Sue look at me in surprise, then back at Teresa who's still sobbing. Pregnant women! Who can figure them out? I let out a relieved laugh.

"Of course he's not dead." Angel chuckles. "I'd swear he waited till she left the building then he just opened his eyes and swore at me."

"How is he?" There's a small crowd gathering around me, throwing questions and pushing to hear the call. I gesture them away.

"His Doctor's on the way to check him out, but he looks okay to me." I can hear Angel smile over the phone. "He's still the bolshy fucker we know and love. Got to go. The Doctor's just arrived. I'll let you know what she says, but I assume you'll be bringing Teresa back to see him."

"Yeah, we'll get there as soon as we can." I reassure him. Closing the phone I look over to Teresa and realize that we might not be there as quickly as I thought.

Teresa's panting heavily and crying that she's wet her pants. Sue laughs at her. "No honey, you've not wet yourself. Your water's just broke." She assures her. *Oh fuck!*

There's no way I can deal with this shit!

"Doc!" I scream at the top of my voice. "Someone go get Doc and get him in here fucking now!" Lucy looks at the panicked expression on my face and the crowd that was pushing for news backs off.

We may be tough bikers, but there's not one of us that wants to stay around for this shit.

Lucy

Sue is talking calmly to Teresa, trying to persuade her to calm her breathing down. She asks her how often the contractions are coming. Teresa didn't need to tell us she was having them, the grimace on her face was enough.

Cowboy is standing there looking lost. He's also looking a little green around the gills truth be told. "Go fetch some towels and hot water." I request. I've no idea if we'll need them or not, but its what they always say in the movies. I'm sure I saw a program once that said they only say it to distract the expectant father and to stop him panicking. He doesn't move, but one of the other guys rushes off to find the stuff for us.

I'm a little concerned that we're not going to be able to get Teresa to the hospital in time. Even if we take her it's a good half hour drive from here. An ambulance would take as long to reach us.

I'm more than relieved when Doc appears on the scene. "Oh, fuck." He mutters under his breath when he sees what's happening.

To his credit he just gets on with it, while Sue is still holding Teresa's hand and trying to calm her down.

Doc asks me to clear the room. I'm able to get everyone to leave apart from Cowboy and Diane. At least Diane might be some use to us, unlike Cowboy. He does however come to his senses and calls Angel. I hear him tell Angel that we might be a little delayed and to cover with Prez.

"I think she's having the baby." He grumbles in response to a question I can't hear. "Yeah. I'll take care of her." He hangs up.

"It's too soon." Teresa wails. She's really distressed. She also looks to be in a shit load of pain the way she's clamping down on Sue's hand. I'm glad that's not my hand she's holding.

"Well apparently your baby decided otherwise." Doc grins at her. "Looks like it's going to be a stubborn bugger like you." He laughs. Teresa doesn't find it funny, instead she gives him a death glare before her features are racked with the pain of another contraction.

"Let's see how far along you are." Doc moves Teresa's skirt out of the way, drawing down her large maternity knickers. Cowboy pales even further when Doc moves his hand in to check how dilated she is.

"I think I need to go check for some more towels." Cowboy gasps before quickly turning on his feet and exiting the room.

"Men!" Sue laughs and I join her.

"Honey, you're almost ready to push." Doc tells Teresa. His voice is calm and gentling. I've only ever heard the gruff way he deals with the guys before so it surprises me.

"I can't have my baby yet. It's too soon. I need Bill." Teresa wails.

"You're going to be fine, and your baby will be fine. We'll have you in that hospital room with Bill before you know it." He soothes her.

The next half hour feels like it drags by. It's heartbreaking hearing the pain in Teresa's voice as she suffers through each contraction. I don't think I want kids if this is how bad it is. I clench my legs together at that thought.

The door opens and a prospect ushers in the very welcome sight of two paramedics. Even Doc looks relieved.

The lead paramedic agrees with Doc that Teresa's too far progressed to risk moving her now. Even though I saw it coming I still gasp at the news she's going to be delivering her baby here in front of me in the clubhouse lounge.

Sue hasn't let go of Teresa's hand the whole time. She's kneeling by her side, wiping her forehead with a damp cloth and whispering words of encouragement in her ear.

"One last push." The paramedic asks of her. "I can see the head crowning now."

Teresa lets out an almighty scream and there's a wush as the baby is delivered into the towel the paramedic has waiting.

There's a hushed silence over the room, there's no sound from the baby and I can't see any movement. This is supposed to be the happiest part of a birth, the time where parents cry with joy and pure happiness. But the father isn't here and I'm crying tears of fear. I'm scared for Teresa and her baby.

"Please God, no." I pray to myself.

The paramedic lifts the baby by its feet and rubs the thick white mucus from its skin. He then hooks a finger in the baby's mouth. It looks brutal and scary, yet none of us question his actions. We just trust that he knows what he's doing whilst praying to God that everything will be okay.

There is no more beautiful sound in the world than the first cry that a baby lets out. I don't think I'll ever forget the moment when I hear the sound break the silence in the room. There's a relieved sigh from everyone in the room. I hear Cowboy mutter "Thank fuck." That was scary.

The second paramedic wraps the baby in a towel and places it on Teresa's chest. "Congratulations." She smiles. "You have a son."

Sue's crying, I'm crying, even Cowboy's crying. He'd rushed into the room at the sound of the baby's first wail. Oddly enough Teresa isn't. Instead she's staring at the tiny bundle in her arms with a mixture of awe and wonder.

"Hello baby." She greets him, placing a soft kiss on his head.

The lead paramedic advises Teresa that she still has to deliver the placenta. He starts to massage her stomach gently to help the process along.

Sue reaches over the baby and places her finger in his tiny hand. "He's beautiful, honey." She smiles. The baby grasps her finger tightly. My heart feels like it's going to break with happiness.

"Say hello to Grandma." Teresa says to her baby. Sue looks at her, obviously shocked at the title.

"But.. what.... " she stutters.

"Sue. You're part of my family and there's nothing I'd like more than for you to be grandmother to my son." She places her hand on top of Sue's. "It's what Dad would have wanted."

"You got a name yet?" The female paramedic asks, busy with her paperwork.

"Yes." Teresa smiles. "It's Aaron Elvis in memory of my Dad." She offers.

Sue sniffles even louder. Cowboy comes up behind me and wraps me in a tight embrace. We both look on at the small family unit in front of us.

After the hell that this club has been through this year I can't think of anything better that could happen to them right now.

"Looks like fate's finally decided to give this club a break." I whisper to Cowboy.

"I hope so." He replies. "I sure fucking hope so."

THE END

Extract from Strip Back by Ava Manello

Prologue

I stand in the bathroom doorway, watching Christy. I love watching her. She's oblivious to my presence. Her head is thrown back, a look of absolute bliss on her face as the water falls on her long, dark tresses before cascading down her back.

Stealthily I move closer, not wanting to draw attention to my presence. I'm enjoying the view far too much to end it just yet. I move closer, staying silent so as not to disturb her.

Through the glass of the shower screen I can see her naked outline. I know she hates it when I stare; she's too conscious of her lumps and bumps as she calls them. I don't see them; instead I see pure perfection. I am mesmerized by the rise and fall of her voluptuous breasts. I watch a trail of water caress her breast, skirting around her nipple, then trailing down over the swell of her stomach, and down. It stays on its path, moving down the curve of her hip, and down her thigh. I love those long legs of hers, whether they're clad in stockings or simply wrapped around me in bed. I watch as the water makes it's final journey and reaches her knee. Fuck. I've made my mind up. I want her. I need her now. My cock is hard as a rock, needing to feel her body against mine.

I step out of my boxers, making my way closer to the shower. The cold air from the door opening startles Christy, but when she sees it's me she relaxes again. The smile that I love spreads over her lips, lighting up her face as she beckons me in with an outstretched finger. I don't hesitate, needing to be with her.

She draws me in until we're both under the blast of hot water. Fuck! How the hell can she stand it this hot? She's a self-confessed shower tart.

She'd be happy to spend all day under the warm stream if I'd let her.

Christy moves for the shower gel, turning me around to lather my back. The slow, sensual stroke of her hands feels so good. The tension starts to leave my shoulders and body.

I turn and lean in to gently nip at her neck, while her hands move behind me to massage my ass. She let's out that little moan that gets me every time. My erection pushes itself into her stomach, wanting in on the action. Laughing quietly she moves a hand around to my front, taking a firm hold of my cock. Shit, that feels so good. She squeezes lightly, massaging up and down my length. Her soap covered hands so soft and slick against me.

I move my head to her breasts, drawing my tongue over her already erect nipple. With the water cascading over my head and shoulders my teeth graze over her nipple, causing her to tighten her grip. Fuck me. I need to be in her. Now.

I turn her quickly so she's facing the wall. Knowing what I want she braces her hands on the shower tiles, pushing her ass out to me. I caress the perfect globes of her ass with my calloused fingers, digging in to leave an imprint.

Trailing my fingers between her legs, I can feel Christy's already wet for me. Thrusting a finger inside her, I cherish the moan that escapes her lips. She pushes her ass further back at me, a silent plea for me to get on with it.

I want to make this moment last, but my cock has other ideas. Removing my fingers I thrust deep inside her. I groan in satisfaction. This is my favorite place, deep inside her, cocooned in her warmth. I hold still, wanting to enjoy the moment as her internal muscles squeeze me firmly, but she has other ideas. She moves against me, bucking her hips and setting the pace. I sense that she needs it hard and fast today, no tender lovemaking. Who am I to deny her?

The water continues to cascade over our bodies as we fuck hard and rough. That's what this is. Pure, animalistic fucking. God, I love fucking her. When we're together like this everything feels right, like it was always meant to be.

She's close, so fucking close I can feel it. I reach for her clit; flicking it viciously. Her resulting orgasm squeezing my cock so tightly I struggle to hold back myself. I thrust as deeply as I can, finding my own release, letting my hot seed fill her

I am in love this woman, the words are on the tip of my tongue to tell her, but I hold back. Unsure if the emotion is shared, if I'm nothing more than a good fuck to her. I've made mistakes in the past, revealed my feelings too soon, and had them thrown back in my face. I need to take my time here. I don't want to be made a fool of again.

My legs are like jelly, but I draw her to me, holding her close. We take our time slowly washing each other down, and enjoying each others bodies, before we head back to my bedroom where we fall asleep spooning each other, naked flesh against naked flesh.

I wake suddenly, and the cold hard realization that this was just a dream hits me. She is gone. I'm alone. The sorrow of my loss hits me harder each time I have the dream, and remember how much she meant to me.

Extract from Heat by K. T. Fisher

Cole slams his mouth against mine and does his delicious growl against my mouth again, which does all sorts of funny things to my body. Mine and Roxie's pleasing sounds mingle together in our quiet home. It doesn't take long until Cole needs more. He wraps his arms around me and picks me up like I don't weigh anything at all. My legs automatically wrap around him as he carries me to the living area. Our mouths are still attacking each other as he sets me down on the sofa.

"How about we give you boys a little something?" I hear Roxie say from the other sofa.

"Hell yeah," Mason growls.

Cole looks up at me. "Let me see that sexy body of yours Lacey."

It's like I want to do anything he wants me to. Without thinking I get up from the sofa and walk to Roxie, who is already standing in the middle of the two sofas. She puts her arms around my shoulders and smiles over at Cole and Mason.

"Lacey and I have had many lonely nights together." She trails her hand softly up the side of my body. She licks my cheek and says, "I love hearing her scream."

I hear Mason groan and I laugh as Roxie slaps my bottom. I trail my finger from her throat and down to the swell of her breasts. "You scream just as loud Rox."

"Fuck." I turn at the sound of Cole. He has his hand on his crotch. I grab a fistful of Roxie's hair and pull it to tilt her head back. She knows exactly what I'm doing and lets her mouth fall open. I lick across her soft lips and then Roxie takes my mouth. We passionately kiss, just like many times before but this time we have two very sexy men watching us. I reach up and grab Roxie's breast, squeezing hard because I know she likes it. I feel a body press against me from behind and I know its Cole. I see Mason turn Roxie around just before Cole turns me to face him. He kisses me wickedly and reaches behind me to unfasten my dress. He pulls the zipper down very slowly kissing along my jaw as he does. His eyes burn me from the inside when he looks at me in my black lacy underwear, then he gives me a very sexy smile. "Lacey in lace."

He takes my bra off from me and rips my thong off my body. If I wasn't so horny I would have complained about my poor thong. Cole captures my mouth with his again and then slowly turns me around to face Roxie, who is now also naked. Roxie winks at me just before we're about to continue our kissing. Roxie's breast is now fully available so when I reach up to touch her again I have full access to her hardened nipple. I glide my thumb over it, teasing her as I stroke my tongue with hers as we kiss. I gasp in her mouth when I feel Roxie's hand between my thighs. She teases my sex with her fingers, spreading my wetness making me even wetter. I can hear Mason and Cole's heavy breathing nearby as they watch my best friend and I play with each other.

"Lie down on the floor." I hear Cole's husky voice in my ear. I do as he says and pull away from Roxie, lying down on the floor. As I lie on my back I lay speechless as Mason sucks my juices from Roxie's fingers. The sight is cruelly erotic and that leaves me squirming.

"Well that's not fair." Cole appears at my feet and kneels down next to them. He places his hands on my knees and slowly opens my legs, spreading them wide. Behind him Mason is now stood behind Roxie with his arms around her, playing with her nipples as they both watch Cole open my legs. I'm so fucking horny right now and I can't tell you how happy I am when Cole finally leans down and swipes his tongue along my wet sex. I close my eyes and I hear Roxie moaning from above me as Cole licks my juices. He only licks me a couple more times when he gets up and looks right at me. "She's all yours now Roxie."

Cole sits on one side of me and Mason on the other as Roxie kneels down and takes Cole's place. With one lick from Roxie I throw my head back on the floor. Roxie dives right in and I close my eyes in bliss. As Roxie brings me closer and closer to the edge I thrash my head from side to side. Mason grabs onto my chin. "Feel it baby."

He kisses me deeply. Being kissed on my mouth and on my sex at the same time is an amazing combination. It's not long until I climax and scream into Mason's mouth.

As I come down from my climax I can hear Roxie moaning. I open my eyes and see that Roxie is now sat on the sofa with her head leaning back as she sighs in pleasure. Mason's head is between her thighs with Roxie's hand gripping his hair. Even though I have just climaxed I'm aroused again at the sight in front of me. Cole begins kissing my neck sending a tingling feeling all over my body. His fingers play with my sex and because I've just orgasmed, I'm extremely sensitive and I can barely take what he's giving me. I close my eyes as the feeling becomes too powerful but Cole stops moving his fingers.

"Open your eyes and watch them and I'll carry on." I try my best to keep my eyes open on the erotic sight. It's unbelievably hard to keep my eyes open while I'm in this much pleasure. I manage to watch Roxie as Mason eats between her thighs, it's not long until I'm screaming another release. I'm shocked to hear that Roxie is screaming along with me.

Who are these men?

They have made us come before they have gotten anything from us. I've never been with a man like this before, usually the guy literally jumps on me when we get to my room and half of the men only care about their selves. They don't seem to care whether I climax or not. I'm sure I will remember this night for as long as I live.

Acknowledgements.

First of all we need to thank our beta team and apologize for the way we cut off chapters in order to gauge a reaction sometimes: Angi, Clare (And her husband M), Emma, Elle, Nadia, Vickie, Ellen, Jane, Clair, Patti and Mel – we thank you for putting up with us and coming back!

To our fantastic street teams who promote us for the love of it, thank you.

To the bloggers who share our teasers, review our books and bring you our new releases – we couldn't do this without you.

And to the readers who enjoy our books – thank you for giving us a reason to keep doing what we love. And thank you especially to those of you who came back after we almost destroyed you in Severed Justice.

Other Books by K.T. Fisher & Ava Manello

K.T. Fisher

Rockstar Daddy (Decoy 1)

Rockstar's Girl (Decoy 2)

Rockstar's Angel (Decoy 3)

Rockstars Valentine (0.5)

Heat (Black Inferno 1)

Ignite (Black Inferno 2)

Ava Manello

Strip Back (Naked Nights 0.5 Eric's Story)

Strip Teaser (Naked Nights 1)

About K.T Fisher

I love reading; it's my favorite hobby. I've always had ideas for my own books packed into my head so I thought I would write them out for people to enjoy

Stalk K.T. Fisher

Facebook:

https://www.facebook.com/pages/KTFisher/49000 3474414733?ref=ts&fref=ts

Twitter:

KTFisher_Author

Goodreads:

https://www.goodreads.com/KTFisher

About Ava Manello

I'm a passionate reader, blogger, publisher, and author. I love nothing more than helping other Indie authors publish their books - be that reviewing, beta reading, formatting or proofreading.

I love erotic suspense that's well written and engages the reader, and I love promoting the heck out of it over on my book blog http://www.kinkybookklub.co.uk

Stalk Ava Manello

Facebook:

http://www.facebook.com/avamanello

Twitter:

@AvaManello

Goodreads:

https://www.goodreads.com/AvaManello

Website:

http://www.avamanello.co.uk